"It's only fair I should offer you the same exit."

"If this is too much to sign on for, say the word," Hayden offered. "Taking on my family drama is a lot to ask of anyone, but especially you."

"I've survived kidnapping and learning I have a whole other family. If any person can take a curve ball, it's me," Tate answered. "If your family's complicated, mine's an unsolvable equation."

"Oh boy. Most complicated one-night stand ever, or the beginning of a future we aren't sure about?"

"Right now I'm taking my life a day at a time. If you're in it, that includes you. So are you? In?"

"And I only have to decide about tonight?"

"Yep. Until tomorrow. And then you'll have another decision to make."

"And we just keep making them day after until...?"

"Until..."

"I can do that."

"Should we seal it with a kiss?"

"At least one."

* * *

Christmas Seduction is part of the Bachelor Pact series.

Dear Reader,

When I initially dreamed up the Bachelor Pact series, *Christmas Seduction* didn't exist! Reid Singleton (from *One Night, White Lies*) had been written as a twin, but I'd decided his brother passed away years ago. Then, my editor said four words that sent my imagination into a free fall: back from the dead.

I'm so, so grateful that my editor was excited about adding a fourth story to the Bachelor Pact lineup! Not only is Tate a back-from-the-dead twin, he's also going to take a trip to London to meet his birth parents for the first time...during Christmas!

I had so much fun researching London at Christmastime. BIG thanks to my new friend and research "partner" Anna, an American living in the UK who gave me lots and lots of details to work with! I was able to pepper in some fun and unique details that absolutely wouldn't be in the book without her. I even purchased English Christmas crackers to share with my family. The wrapped poppers were a huge hit!

Another fun aspect I included in Tate and Hayden's story was the wellness community that Tate owns and runs. After a trip to a similar community outside Atlanta, Georgia, called Serenbe, I couldn't resist the lush and peaceful setting for my developer hero and my yoga instructor heroine. I hope you enjoy Tate and Hayden's story. If you do, I'd love to hear from you at jessica@jessicalemmon.com.

Happy reading!

Jessica xo

JESSICA LEMMON

CHRISTMAS SEDUCTION

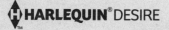

Recycling programs
for this product may
not exist in your area.

ISBN-13: 978-1-335-60393-7

Christmas Seduction

Copyright © 2019 by Jessica Lemmon

This is a work of fiction. Names, characters, places and incidents are either the product of the author's imagination or are used fictitiously, and any resemblance to actual persons, living or dead, business establishments, events or locales is entirely coincidental.

This edition published by arrangement with Harlequin Books S.A.

For questions and comments about the quality of this book, please contact us at CustomerService@Harlequin.com.

Printed in U.S.A.

HARLEQUIN®
www.Harlequin.com

A former job-hopper, **Jessica Lemmon** resides in Ohio with her husband and rescue dog. She holds a degree in graphic design currently gathering dust in an impressive frame. When she's not writing supersexy heroes, she can be found cooking, drawing, drinking coffee (okay, wine) and eating potato chips. She firmly believes God gifts us with talents for a purpose, and with His help, you can create the life you want.

Jessica is a social media junkie who loves to hear from readers. You can learn more at jessicalemmon.com.

Books by Jessica Lemmon

Harlequin Desire

Dallas Billionaires Club

Lone Star Lovers
A Snowbound Scandal
A Christmas Proposition

The Bachelor Pact

Best Friends, Secret Lovers
Temporary to Tempted
One Night, White Lies
Christmas Seduction

Visit her Author Profile page at Harlequin.com, or jessicalemmon.com, for more titles.

You can find Jessica Lemmon on Facebook, along with other Harlequin Desire authors, at Facebook.com/harlequindesireauthors!

For all my friends at the lake—you are the embodiment of a true community, and I'm so blessed to know you.

One

Outside the Brass Pony, a five-star restaurant where he'd nursed more than one whiskey at the bar, Tate Duncan stood beneath the canopy and watched the rain come down in sheets.

He'd picked a hell of a night to walk.

But, that's the way the streets here were designed in Spright Wellness Community. With plenty of side-walks and paths cutting through the woods, making a walk more convenient than a winding car ride to your destination. This was a wellness community, after all.

Tate and a dedicated team of contractors had developed the health and wellness community five years ago. Its location? Spright Island, an enviable utopia thirty-minutes by ferry from Seattle, Washington, and Tate's twenty-fifth birthday gift from his adoptive parents. The island had been, and remained, a nature preserve and was the perfect spot to build a sustainable, peaceful, modern neighborhood that would attract curious city dwellers.

He'd imagined into existence the luxury wellness enclave, which had become a refuge of sorts for those who desired a strong sense of community, and wanted to be surrounded by lush greenery rather than concrete. As a result, Spright Wellness Community teemed with residents who glowed with wealth and stank of wellness. There was a big demand to live small and, even though it wasn't all that small, SWC had that feel about it.

"Umbrella, Mr. Duncan?" The manager of the Brass Pony, Jared Tomalin, leaned out the door and offered a black umbrella by it's U-shaped handle. His smile faded much as it had earlier when he'd attempted to make small talk and learned that "Mr. Duncan" wasn't in the mood for small talk tonight.

There had been a time, and it wasn't that long ago, that Tate would have turned, given Jared a smile and accepted the offer, saying, "Thank you. I'll bring it back by tomorrow." Now, he gave the manager a withering glare and stalked off into the abysmal weather. A twenty-minute jaunt—soggy, chilling and wet—was a good metaphor for the downward spiral his life had taken recently.

Everything in Tate's world had been on an upward track, steady and stable until…

Until.

He popped his collar and tucked his hands into the pockets of his leather jacket. Chin down, eyes on the gathering puddles under his feet, he began to walk.

Surrounding neighborhoods were marked by a variety of shops; markets with fresh produce and organic goods, restaurants like the Pony with reputations that drew diners from the coast, plus plenty of service-based businesses like salons, art stores and yoga studios. With its high-end wellness fare, SWC was part luxury living, part hippie commune, but to Tate, simply home.

A rare flash of headlights caught his attention and he lifted his head. Summer's Market stood on the opposite side of the street, the wooden shelves and brightly-colored stacks of produce visible from the windows. The safety lights spotlighted wheels of cheese and boxed crackers arranged near a selection of wine. It was hard to believe he'd once had nothing better to do than pop into Summer's for a wine-tasting and cheese-pairing and have a chat with his neighbors.

Back when I knew who I was.

Tate had never thought of identity as a wily thing, but lately his own had been wriggling, slippery in his grip. He'd known once, with certainty, who he was: the son of William and Marion Duncan, from California. Life, apparently, had other plans for him. Plans that had sent him careening, grappling to understand how he'd *become* the son of William and Marion Duncan, right around the same time the woman who was supposed to marry him had walked away.

I can't do this, Tate, Claire had told him, her delicate features screwed into an expression of regret. Then she'd given back the engagement ring. That was two weeks ago. Since then, he'd become a ripe bastard.

The rhythm of his breath paced the time along with

his steps. Rainwater beat drumlike on his head and soaked into his Italian leather shoes.

On his side of the street, he came upon a building that held an array of businesses, including an acupuncture office, a family doctor and a yoga studio. The yoga studio was the only one lit inside, by a pair of pink hued salt lamps glowing warmly on top of a desk. He peered through the window, wishing he'd have accepted the damn umbrella. Wishing he could absorb the warmth emitting from the place. It was orderly, homey, with its scarred wooden floors and stacks of cubbies for storing shoes and cell phones during class.

He'd been inside once before, to greet the new owner who'd leased the space. Yoga by Hayden was run by Hayden Green, a new resident who'd been in SWC a little over a year now. He saw her around town sometimes. She was the equivalent of looking at the sun. Bright, glowing, joyful. She had a skip in her step and a smile on her face most days. He wondered if yoga was her secret to being happy, if maybe he should try it—make that his new therapy. God knew he wasn't heading back to Dr. Schroder any time soon.

The first-world problems he used to bring to his therapist were laughable considering the *actual* drama surrounding him now. He could imagine that conversation, his doc's eyebrows climbing her forehead into her coifed dark hair.

Yeah, so I found out I was kidnapped when I was three, adopted out for a large sum of money and my real parents live in London. No, my adoptive parents didn't know I was kidnapped. Yes, London. Oh, and I have a brother. We're twins.

Eerie. That's what this was. Like a scary story told around a campfire, there was a large chunk of him that wanted to believe it was false. That the repressed memory of big hands cuffing him under the arms and dragging him away from his and his twin brother's birthday party had been a nightmare he could awaken from. That George and Jane Singleton were no more related to him than the Queen of England.

Though he was from the UK, so God help him, he *could be* related to the Queen of England.

Ice-cold raindrops soaked through his hair to his scalp, and he shuddered. His mind had been bobbing in the atmosphere like a lost balloon for going on two months now. He wasn't sure he'd ever get back to normal at this rate. Wasn't sure if he knew what normal *was* any longer.

This entire situation was surreal. And after living an organized, regimented, successful life, a shock he hadn't been prepared to deal with.

What were the odds of two estranged London-born twin brothers bumping into each other in a Seattle coffee shop nearly thirty years later?

Astronomical.

He let out a fractured laugh. "You're not well enough to be in a wellness community."

Overhead, he admired a streetlamp like the others lining the sidewalks, remembering how a formerly sane version of himself had commissioned a welder to design them. They resembled tree branches, complete with curling leaves along the top, the lights encased in a bell-shaped flower. Tate mused that they had a fairy-tale quality. Like that smoking caterpillar or the

Cheshire cat from *Alice in Wonderland* could appear perched on one at any moment.

"You're losing it, Duncan."

But his smile was short-lived when he abruptly remembered that he wasn't a Duncan. Not really.

He was a Singleton.

Whatever the hell that meant.

The sharp whistle of the teakettle pulled Hayden Green's attention from her book. She made the short trek to her kitchen, flipped the gas burner off and reached for her waiting teacup.

Through the driving rain, she could barely make out the shape of the market across the street and yet her senses prickled. Stepping closer to her upstairs window, she squinted at the street below and found her senses were, as usual, spot-on.

In the deluge lurked a figure. Right outside her yoga studio. It was a man, most definitely, his dark leather jacket unable to hide the breadth of his shoulders.

She pressed her forehead against the pane to get a better look, confident he couldn't see her since the kitchen light was off. He tilted his head back; the street light overhead illuminating him as the rain splashed his upturned face and closed eyelids.

Hayden recognized her unexpected visitor instantly. "Tate Duncan, what are you doing?"

Tate's reputation had reached almost mythical proportions on Spright Island. He owned the island, so everyone knew him or knew *of him*, anyway. Hayden was somewhere in between. She knew of him—of his legendary pushbacks on the laws that stated their community had to have standard streetlamps and ugly yellow concrete curbs. Tate had fought for, and won, the right to design streetlamps that were art sculptures and to install curbs of sparkling quartz. He'd personally overseen every detail because to him, the details mattered.

Hayden had been romanced by SWC. It was a relaxing, serene place to live—a retreat from bustling city life. She had been born in Seattle into a busy, distracting, dysfunctional household, and had longed her entire adult life to be somewhere less busy and distracting.

When she'd learned about Spright Island's wellness community a year and a half ago, she'd come to visit. Days later, she'd taken out as big a business loan as the bank would give her and leased the space for her yoga studio. She'd quit her job at the YMCA, finagled her way out of her Seattle apartment's lease and moved here with minimal belongings.

It'd been her fresh start.

Shortly after, Tate had stopped by her studio to personally welcome her to the neighborhood and invite her to a wine tasting happening that weekend at Summer's Market. It was a kindness she hadn't expected, and without it, she might never have met and grown to know her neighbors.

She rarely saw a suit and tie step foot into a yoga studio, so Tate's presence had garnered every ounce of her attention. One of his signature quick, potent smiles later, she'd promptly lost any train of thought she'd had. As it turned out, the legendary Tate Duncan was also stupidly attractive, and when he smiled, that attractiveness doubled.

She'd grown used to his presence around town, if not his mind-numbing male beauty. She and Tate had bumped into each other several times in town, from the market to the restaurant to her favorite café. He'd always offered a smile and asked her how the studio was doing. Come to think of it, it'd been a while since she'd spoken to him. She'd seen him in recent weeks— *or was that a month ago?*—when she'd left the post office. He'd had his cell phone to his ear and was talking to someone, a deep frown marring his perfect brow.

He'd scanned the road and she'd waved when his eyes reached her, but he didn't react at all, only kept talking on the phone. It was strange behavior for Tate, but she'd written it off.

But now, watching him stand in the rain and willingly get soaked, she wondered if his behavior that day had been strange after all. She glanced over at her teakettle, considering. It wouldn't hurt to invite him in for a cup…

Once he'd gone out of his way to make her feel welcome. The least she could do was offer him a friendly ear to bend. Just in case he needed one.

She bypassed her front door for the door next to her coat closet. It led to a private staircase and down to her yoga studio. She shared the building with a few other businesses, but her apartment was in a hallway all its own. The attached studio and private entryway were her favorite aspects of the unique building.

Downstairs, she flipped on the studio's overhead lights and Tate blinked over at her, recognition dawning. He lifted a hand in a semblance of a wave, like he was embarrassed to be caught outside her place of business.

The stirring of her senses reinforced her instincts to come down here. Tate needed someone to talk to even more than he needed a warm space to dry off.

She unlocked the door and held it open for him, tipping her head to invite him in. "Wet night for a walk."

He ran a hand through his soaking hair and offered a chagrined twist of his lips, a far cry from the genuine smile he'd given her almost every other time she'd seen him.

He wore dark pants and shoes, his leather coat zipped to his chin. Her day had been packed with errands, so she still wore her jeans and soft, cream-colored sweater from earlier. If she'd greeted him wearing her usual—leggings and slouchy sweatshirt, minus the bra—he wouldn't have been the only one of them embarrassed.

"My teakettle whistled and then I spotted you down here. You look like you could use a warm drink."

"Do I?" He palmed his neck and glanced behind him. Maybe she'd misread this situation after all.

"Unless you're waiting for someone?"

She'd seen him in town with a waifish blonde woman a handful of times. *Claire*, Hayden had gleaned. Tate's girlfriend and very recently, fiancée. The other woman seemed proper and rigid, and Hayden's first thought was that she was an odd match for the always bright and cheery Tate...though he wasn't bright or cheery at the moment.

"No. I was at the Pony," he said of the restaurant up the hill from here. "The rain caught me."

"I'd offer to drive you home, but I don't have a car." One of the luxuries she'd given up to afford to move to Spright Island, but the sacrifice had been worth it. *Peace* had been worth it.

Every shop or store in the community could be reached on foot if she planned ahead, and she had a few friends in the area or could call a car service if she needed to venture farther.

"But I do have tea." She opened the door wider.

"Of course. Thank you." He stepped into the studio, his shoes squishing on her welcome mat. "Sorry about this."

"No worries." She locked the door behind him and grabbed a towel from a nearby cabinet. "Clean, fluffy towel? They're for my hot yoga classes."

He accepted with a nod and sopped the water from his hair.

"Tea's in my apartment." She gestured to the open doorway leading upstairs. "Don't worry about wet shoes. I'm not that formal."

Tate followed her upstairs and inside her *blessedly spotless* apartment. She'd cleaned yesterday. She was fairly tidy, but some weeks got the best of her and she didn't get around to vacuuming or changing her sheets.

By the time he was in the center of her living room and she was shutting the door to the staircase behind her, she was questioning her invitation.

A man in her apartment shrank it down until it felt like she lived in a cereal box—and this man in particular infused the immediate space with a sizzling attraction she'd felt since he first shook her hand.

Hayden Green, he'd said. *You have the perfect last name for this community.*

Now, he pegged her with a look that could only be described as vulnerable, as if something was really, *really* off. She wanted nothing more than to cross the room and scoop him into her arms. But she couldn't do that. He had a fiancée. And she wasn't looking for a romantic relationship.

No matter how hot he was.

"Tea," she reminded herself and then stepped around him to walk to the kitchen.

Two

Tate slipped out of his leather jacket and hung it on an honest-to-goodness coatrack in between the door and the television. His shirt beneath was dry, thank goodness, and his pants were in the process of drying, but he kicked off his shoes rather than track puddles through Hayden's apartment.

Since he'd personally approved the design of every structure in SWC, he knew this building. He'd expected her place to be both modern and cozy, but she'd added her own sense of unique style. Much like Hayden herself, her apartment was laid-back with a Zen feel. From the live potted plants near the window to the black-and-white woven rug on the floor. A camel-brown sofa stood next to a coffee table, its surface cluttered with books. Oversize deep gold throw pillows were stacked on the floor for sitting, a journal and a pen resting on top of one of them.

"I like what you've done with the place." He was still drying his hair with the towel when he leaned forward to study the photos on the mantel above a gas fireplace. He'd expected family photos, maybe one of a boyfriend, or a niece or nephew. Instead the frames held quotes. One of them was the silhouette of a woman in a yoga pose with wording underneath that read, *I bend so I don't break*, and the other a plain black background with white lettering: *If you stumble, make it part of the dance.*

"Do you have a tea preference?" she called from the kitchen.

"Not really."

He didn't drink tea, though he supposed he should, since he'd recently learned he was *from fucking London.*

"I have green, peppermint and chai. Green has caffeine, so let's not go there." She peeked at him before tucking the packet back into the drawer like she'd intuited a pending breakdown.

Great. Nothing like an emasculating bout of anxiety to finish up his day.

"Peppermint would be good if you were nauseous or ate too much, and chai will warm you up." She narrowed her eyes, assessing him anew. "Chai."

"Chai's fine. Thanks again."

She set about making his tea and he watched her, the fluid way she moved as she hummed to herself in the small kitchen. Stepping into Hayden's apartment was a lot like stepping into a therapist's office, only not as stuffy. As if being in her space tempted him to open up. Whether it was the rich, earthy colors or the offer of a soothing, hot drink he didn't know. Maybe both.

He was surprised she'd invited him in, considering she'd found him standing in a downpour staring blankly at the window.

Probably he should get around to addressing that.

She set the mugs on the coffee table, and he moved to the sofa, debating whether or not to sit.

"You're dry enough," she said, reading his mind. She swiped the towel and disappeared into the bedroom before coming back out. Her walk was as confident as they came, with an elegance reminding him of Claire.

Claire. Her last words to him two weeks ago kept him awake at night, along with the other melee of crap bouncing around in his head.

I can't handle this right now, Tate. I have a job. A life. Let's have a cooling-off period. I'm sure you'd like some time alone.

He felt alone, more alone than ever now that the holidays were coming up. His adoptive parents were fretting, though he tried to reassure them. Nothing would reassure his mother, he knew. Guilt was a carnivorous beast.

Hayden lit a candle on a nearby shelf, and he took back his earlier comparison to Claire. Hayden was completely different. From her dark hair to her curvy dancer's body.

Pointing to the quote on the mantel, he said, "I bet you've never stumbled a day in your life."

With a smile, she sat next to him and lifted her mug. "I've stumbled many times. Do you know how hard it is to do a headstand in yoga?"

"How is the studio doing? I was considering trying a class." A clumsy segue, but that might explain why he'd been lingering outside like a grade A creeper. "I've been…stressed. I thought yoga might be a good de-stressor."

"Yoga's a *great* de-stressor," she said conversationally, as if him coming to this conclusion while standing in a downpour was normal. "I teach scheduled group classes as well as private sessions."

"One on one?" He'd bet her schedule was packed. Being in her presence for a few minutes had already made him feel more relaxed.

"Yep. A lot of people around here prefer one-on-one help with their practice. Others just like being alone with no help at all, which is why I open the space for members once a week."

"That's a lot of options." She must work around the clock.

"There are a lot of people here, or haven't you noticed, Mr. Spright Island?" She winked, thick dark lashes closing over one chocolate-brown iris. Had she always been this beautiful?

"I noticed." He returned her smile. There were just shy of nine hundred houses in SWC. That made for plenty of residents milling around town and, more often than he was previously aware, apparently in Hayden's yoga studio.

"I don't believe you want to talk about yoga." Her gaze was a bare lightbulb on a string over his head, as if there was no way to hide what had been rattling around in his brain tonight. She lifted dark, inquisitive eyebrows. "You look like you have something interesting to talk about."

The pull toward her was real and raw—the realest sensation he'd felt in a while. It grounded him, grabbed him by the balls and demanded his full attention.

"I didn't plan on talking about it…" he admitted, but she must have heard the ellipsis at the end of that sentence.

She tilted her head, sage interest in whatever he might say next. Wavy dark brown hair surrounded a cherubic heart-shaped face, her deep brown eyes at once tender and inviting. *Inviting.* There was that word again. Unbidden, his gaze roamed over her tanned skin, her V-necked collar and delicate collarbone. How had he not noticed before? She was *alarmingly* beautiful.

"I'm sorry." Her palm landed on his forearm. "I'm prying. You don't have to say anything."

She moved to pull her hand away but he captured her fingers in his, studying her shiny, clear nails and admiring the olive shade of her skin and the way her hand offset his own pinker hue.

"There are aspects of my life I was certain of a month and a half ago," he said, idly stroking her hand with his thumb. "I was certain that my parents' names were William and Marion Duncan." He offered a sad smile as Hayden's eyebrows dipped in confusion. "I suppose they technically still are my parents, but they're also not. I'm adopted."

Her plush mouth pulled into a soft frown, but she didn't interrupt.

"I recently learned that the agency—" *or more accurately, the kidnappers* "—lied about my birth parents. Turns out they're alive and living in London. And I have a brother." He paused before clarifying, "A twin brother."

Hayden's lashes fluttered. "Wow."

"Fraternal, but he's a good-looking bastard."

She squeezed his fingers. There for him in spite of owing him nothing. That should've been Claire's job.

"I was certain that I was the owner/operator of Spright Island's premier, thriving wellness community," he stated in his radio-commercial voice. "That, thank God, hasn't changed. SWC is a sanctuary of sorts. There is a different vibe here that you can't find inland."

"I know exactly what you mean. I stepped foot in my studio downstairs that first time, and it had this positive energy about it. Does that sound unbelievable?"

No more unbelievable than being kidnapped in another country and having no memory of it.

"It doesn't sound unbelievable." He took pride in what he'd built. He'd poured himself, body and soul, into what he created, so it wasn't surprising some of that had leaked into the energy of this place.

"I was also certain I was going to be married to Claire Waterson."

At the mention of a fiancée, Hayden tugged her hand from his and wrapped her fingers around her mug. He didn't think it was because she was thirsty.

"When I found out about my family tree, she bailed on me," he told her. "I didn't expect that."

He raked his hands through his damp hair, unable to stop the flow of words now that he'd undammed them. "You invited me in for tea thinking I had something on my mind. Bet you didn't expect a full-blown identity crisis."

Her eyebrows dipped in sympathy.

"I just need… I need…" Dropping his head in his hands, he trailed off, muttering to the floor, "Christ, I have no idea what I need."

He felt the couch shift and dip, and then Hayden's hand was on his back, moving in comforting circles.

"I've had my share of family drama, trust me. But nothing like what you're going through. It's okay for you to feel unsure. Lost."

He faced her. This close, he could smell her soft lavender perfume and see the gold flecks in her dark eyes. He hadn't planned on coming here, or on sitting on her couch and spilling his heart out. He and Hayden were *friendly*, not friends. But her comforting touch on his back, the way her words seemed to soothe the recently broken part of him…

Maybe what he needed was *her*.

He leaned forward, his eyes focused on her mouth and the satisfaction kissing her would bring.

"Tate." She jerked away, sobering him instantly.

"Sorry. I'm sorry." What the hell was he thinking? That Hayden invited him in to make out on her couch? That sharing his sob story would somehow turn her on? As if any woman wanted to be with a man who was in pieces.

He stood to leave. She stood with him.

"Listen, Tate—"

"I shouldn't have come here." He pulled his coat on and shoved his feet in his shoes, grateful for the leather slip-ons. At least there wouldn't be an awkward interlude while he tied his laces. "Thank you for listening. I'm really very sorry."

"Wait." She arrived at the coatrack as he was stuffing his arms into his still-wet leather coat.

"I'm going to go." He turned to apologize again, but was damn near knocked off his feet when Hayden pushed to her toes, cuffed the back of his neck and pulled his mouth down to hers.

Three

Hayden had fantasized of kissing Tate ever since she first laid eyes on him. She knew he wasn't meant to be hers in real life, but in her fantasies, well, there were no rules.

Of all the imagined kisses they'd shared, none compared to the actual kiss she was experiencing now.

The moment their lips touched, he grabbed on to her like a lifeline, eagerly plunging his tongue into her mouth. His skin was chilly from the rain, but his body radiated heat. She was downright toasty in his arms… and getting hotter by the second.

She tasted dark liquor—bourbon or whiskey—on his tongue, but there was a tinge of something else. Sadness, if she wasn't mistaken. Sadness over learning he had a brother after all these years—a twin brother. Wow, that was wild…

A pair of strong hands gripped her waist. Tate tugged her close, and when her breasts flattened against his chest all other thoughts flew from her head. The water clinging to his coat soaked through her sweater, causing her nipples to bead to tight peaks inside her bra.

Still, she kissed him.

She wasn't done with this real-life fantasy. A brief thought of Claire Waterson crashed into her mind, and she shoved it out. They were broken up—he'd said so himself. Hayden had nothing to feel guilty about.

Besides, he needed her. Whenever she'd been lost or sad, she'd taken solace in her friends. That was what she offered to him now.

A safe space.

She pulled her lips from Tate's to catch her breath, her mind buzzing and her limbs vibrating. His chest and shoulders rose and fell, the hectic rhythm set by the brief make-out session. An unsure smile tilted his mouth, and she returned it with one of her own.

"Better?" she asked.

His low laugh soaked into her like rum on sponge-cake. He pulled his hand over his mouth and then back through his hair, and her knees nearly gave way. It'd be so easy to lean in and taste him again, to offer her body as a place for him to lay his worries…

"I didn't mean to take advantage of your hospitality. Honest." His blue eyes shimmered in the candlelight.

"You didn't. I always serve tea with French kisses. It's a package deal."

"The best deal in town," he murmured. He stroked her jaw tenderly, those tempting lips offering the sincerest "thank you" she'd ever heard.

"Call a car," she said, before she asked him to stay. "It's pouring out there."

"Actually—" he opened the door that led down to her studio "—I could use a cool, brisk walk after that kiss."

She smiled, pleased. It wasn't every day she could curl a hot guy's toes. She considered this rare feat a victory.

"I'll lock the studio door behind me. There are some real weirdos out there…"

She grinned, knowing he was referring to himself.

Before he pulled the door shut, he stuck his head through the crack. "You don't really kiss everyone you offer tea, do you?"

"Wouldn't you like to know." She was tempted to put another brief peck on his mouth, but he disappeared through the gap before she could. A fraction of a second later, she was looking at the wood panel instead of his handsome face and wondering if she'd hallucinated the entire thing.

"Hayden, Hayden," she chastised gently as she engaged the lock and drew the chain. She turned and eyed the mugs of tea, Tate's untouched and hers barely drunk. His lips hadn't so much as grazed the edge of that mug.

But they were all over yours.

That spontaneous kiss had rocked her world.

She dashed to the window and peered out into the rain, hoping for one more glance at her nighttime visitor. A dark figure passed under a streetlamp, his shoulders under his ears, his hair wet all over again. Before he disappeared from sight, he turned to face her building and walked a few steps backward. She couldn't see his face from that far away, but she liked to believe he was smiling.

She touched her lips.

So was she.

Three wet days later, the rain had downgraded from downpour to light drizzle. Even walking across the street to Summer's Market yesterday for ingredients for blueberry muffins had left Hayden wet and cold. She'd returned home soaked to the bone, her hair smelling of rainwater.

Which, of course, reminded her of *The Kiss* from the other day. She hadn't seen Tate since. Not that she'd expected him to stop by, but… Well, was *hope* the wrong word to use?

Over and over, she'd remembered the feel of Tate's firm lips, his capable hands gripping her hips, the vulnerability in his smile. The ways his eyes shined with curiosity afterward.

Knowing she'd erased some of his sadness made her feel special. She was beginning to think she actually *missed him*. Odd, considering the concept of missing him was foreign until that kiss.

The chilly bite of the wind cut through her puffy, lightweight coat, and she tucked her chin behind the zipped collar as she crossed the street to the café.

Nothing better for walking off sexual frustration than a brisk November stroll.

She had an advanced yoga class in an hour and was tired just thinking about it. A hot cup of coffee would put some much-needed pep in her step.

She wasn't the only resident of SWC taking advantage of the drier weather. Cold drizzles they were willing to brave. Drenching downpours, not so much. As a result, there was a buzz in the air, an audible din of chatter amongst the couples or single professionals lounging in the outdoor patio. It was closed off for the winter, the temporary walls and tall gas heaters making the space warm enough for the overflow of customers.

Inside, Hayden rubbed her hands together, delighted to find that the person in line ahead of her was finished ordering. The only thing better than a Sprightly Bean coffee at the start of a day was not waiting in line to get one. She ordered a large caramel latte and stepped to the side to wait. Not thirty seconds into her studying the glass case of doughnuts and other sinful baked goods, the low voice from her dreams spoke over her shoulder.

"I've seen regret before, and it looks a lot like the expression on your face, Ms. Green."

Her smile crested her mouth before she turned. She thought she was prepared to come face-to-face with Tate until she did. His dark wool coat was draped over a charcoal-gray suit, his hair neatly styled against his head and slightly damp, she guessed from a recent shower. And wasn't that a pleasant image? Him naked, water flowing over lean muscle, corded forearms, long, strong legs...

"Am I broadcasting regret?" she asked, her voice a flirty lilt.

He pointed at the bakery case. "Was it the éclair or the lemon–poppy seed muffin that caused it?"

"Hmm." She pretended to consider. "I could be regretting my impulsive behavior three days ago."

His eyebrows rose like she'd stunned him. She wasn't much of a wallflower, which he should know after she'd grabbed him up and kissed him.

He opened his mouth to reply when a thin blonde woman glided around the corner, tugging a glove onto her hand. *Claire.*

"I'm ready to go," she announced without preamble. Or manners. Or delicacy.

As if her frosty entrance had chilled them both, Hayden's smile vanished and Tate retreated.

He nodded at Claire Waterson, his frown appearing both on his mouth and forehead. "Hayden, this is Claire. Claire, this is Hayden Green. She owns the yoga studio down the road."

"Charmed." Claire nodded curtly as she tugged on her other glove. No offer of a handshake, but Hayden didn't want to shake the other woman's hand, anyway.

"See you around," Tate told Hayden.

She watched them leave, her forehead scrunching when Tate touched Claire's back on the walk out to a car. He hadn't walked to the café today. Hayden would bet *Priss in Boots* hadn't allowed it.

"Grande caramel latte." The cheery barista handed over Hayden's coffee, and she managed a genial smile before walking out the front door, her steps heavy. Tate, in the driver's seat, pulled away from the curb on the opposite side of the street. He didn't wave, but did manage a compressed half smile.

While Hayden didn't have any claim on him, she'd admit she felt like an idiot for believing him. He'd sounded so sincere when he said his relationship with Claire was over. Or had he implied it was over? Either way, if she'd had any idea Tate and Claire would be sharing morning coffee a few days later, Hayden never would have kissed him. From the looks of it, he and Claire were very much *together*.

Ew.

She started her march home, an unhealthy dose of anger seeping into her bloodstream. The first sip of her coffee burned her tongue, and the wind blew directly into her face, cold and bitter.

A series of beeps sounded from her pocket and Hayden's back stiffened. That was her mother's ringtone. It never failed to cause a cocktail of panic, fear and resentment to boil over. She ignored the second ring and then the third and, a minute later, the chime of her voice mail.

When Hayden left Seattle, it had felt like more of an escape. Her mother had been—and was still—stressed to the max, refusing to draw boundary lines around the one woman causing problems in their lives: Hayden's alcoholic grandmother. Grandma Winnie favored drama and bottom-shelf vodka in equal measures, and Hayden's mother, Patti, had turned codependency into an art form. Hayden's dad, Glenn, was content to let the matriarchs rule the roost, as if he'd eschewed himself from the chaos in the only way he knew how: silence.

After years of trying to balance family drama with her own desperate need for stability, Hayden left Seattle and her family behind for the oasis of Spright Island.

By the time she was changing for her class, her coffee was cool and her mind was numb. She paused in the living room of her apartment, put her hands over her heart and took three deep breaths.

There was no sense in being angry at Grandma Winnie for being an alcoholic. It wasn't her fault she had a disease. Similarly, she let go of worrying over her mother's codependence and her father's blind eye.

"Everyone is doing the best they can," she said aloud.

But as she trotted down the stairs to the studio and unlocked the door for a few waiting guests, she found that there was one person in her life she didn't feel as magnanimous toward.

The man who'd kissed her soundly, scrambled her senses and then showed up in town with the very woman he claimed had left him behind.

"Hi, Hayden," greeted Jan, the first of her students through the door.

Hayden returned Jan's smile and shoved aside her tumultuous thoughts. She owed it to her class to be present and bring good energy, not bad.

Family drama— and Tate drama—would be waiting for her when the class was over, whether she wanted it or not.

Four

The bell over her studio entrance jangled as Hayden's evening class filed out of the building. She was behind the desk, jotting down a note for Marla, who'd been coming for individual classes but decided tonight she wanted to join the group. Since Marla hadn't brought her credit card, Hayden had promised to email her in the morning.

Hayden stuck a reminder Post-it note onto the cover of her hardbound planner and looked up, expecting to see the last of her students leave. Instead, someone was coming *in*.

A certain someone who hadn't left her mind no matter how hard she tried to stop thinking about him.

Dressed in black athletic pants and a long-sleeved black T-shirt, Tate shrugged out of the same leather jacket he'd worn the night they kissed. It'd been five days since that kiss. Two days since the coffee shop.

She still wasn't happy with him, but it was impossible not to admire his exquisite hotness.

"Hey," she blurted, unsure what else to say.

"Hey." He looked over his shoulder. "I know I missed class, but I was hoping to schedule a one-on-one."

Her mind went to the last "one-on-one" session they'd had. She hadn't forgotten that kiss. She probably never would. It was burned onto her frontal lobe.

"Individual sessions have to be scheduled ahead of time," she said as tartly as she could manage. The vision of him with Claire was too fresh in her mind for her to be cordial.

"Are you sure?" He tilted his head as he stepped closer to her.

"If you're here because you feel you owe me an explanation or you need to air your regrets—"

"No. Nothing like that."

She lifted her eyebrows, asking a silent *well?*

"I haven't been in control of my life lately. Everything's moving at warp speed, and I'm caught in the undertow. You ever feel like you've lost control? Once upon a time you had it in your hands, and now..." He looked down at his own fists gripping his coat as his mouth pulled down at the corners.

She knew exactly what that was like, but in reverse order. Her world had been moving at warp speed since birth, and only moving to SWC had stopped its trajectory.

She sympathized with Tate, though she was tempted to cut her losses and show him the door.

"And taking a yoga class with me would help you feel in control?" she asked anyway.

"Ah, well. Not exactly." Palm on his neck, he studied the floor and then peeked up at her with a look of chagrin so magnetic, her heart skipped a beat. "I'm really good at turning you on. At least I think I would be. Are you still doling out kisses with every cup of tea?"

She gripped the edge of the front desk, digesting what he'd just said. He *was* good at turning her on. She knew that, but what was she supposed to do with it? Especially when Tate stood in front of her looking coy and cunning and yet vulnerable and was offering… Wait… Was this *a booty call*?

"Sorry. That offer expired." Not that she was above kissing him, but… "I'm not going to be your girl on the side, Tate. What would Claire say?"

"That's over. It's *been* over. What you saw at the coffee shop was her finalizing things. You know, like you do after someone dies."

He paced to the salt lamp on her desk and stared at it for a beat. "She dropped off a box of my stuff at my house and then asked if we could grab a coffee and talk. I told her she could talk to me there, but she said she preferred neutral territory."

"Oh." It was a breakup. Hayden had misread that entire exchange. Still… "And you didn't feel the need to explain yourself after I saw you at the café? You thought you'd instead come here and…" She waved a hand uselessly, unable to finish her thought, since she wasn't 100 percent sure why he was here.

"I thought we could start with a yoga session." He dipped his chin. "If you have any openings for, say, now."

She tried to tell him no, but found she couldn't. Tate Duncan didn't have to work hard to charm her on any given day, and today he was actually trying.

"How about..." She flipped open her planner and traced her finger down the page. "Tomorrow. Noon."

"Deal."

"I'll need your credit card. I require a nonrefundable down payment for the first appointment."

"Smart."

She hummed. She wasn't so sure this was smart, but was too curious to turn him away.

The morning of his yoga appointment, Tate set out for Hayden's studio. The day was dry if chilly, but he welcomed the burning cold in his lungs as he cut through a path in the woods.

He'd been out for a quick trip to Summer's Market when he'd witnessed Hayden's evening class letting out. He hadn't planned on walking across the street and inside, but when he found himself in front of her, he had to have a reason for being there.

Besides the obvious.

Hayden had consumed damn near every one of his waking thoughts, which was a relief compared to his usual pastime: turning over his parentage, the truth about where he came from, or the disastrous outcome since.

He'd blamed the kiss on whiskey and a need for connection. The liquor buzz was long gone, but the imprint of her kiss remained like a brand. It was reckless to leap into the flames after he'd just escaped a fire—

Claire should've rendered him numb. But Hayden… she was different.

Not only had she been there for him when he'd been adrift on his own, but she replaced his tumultuous thoughts with something a hell of a lot better.

Sex.

He wanted her. He wanted her in his arms and in his bed. He wanted her moaning beneath him, her nails scratching down his back.

It was as if he'd devolved to his most carnal desires when she was around, and for a change, he was all for it. He was tired of feeling unmoored, helpless. Sad. With her he felt strong, capable. She'd come apart in his arms during that kiss. She may have put him through his paces last night, but he respected her for it.

Hell, he knew he'd stepped in it with Hayden the moment he left that café with Claire. But he'd owed Claire that meeting. They'd dated for three years and had been recently engaged, though he now wondered if that was more of a technicality. She'd never lived with him—never wanted to. She didn't treasure Spright Island or his community the way he did.

The way Hayden does. That kiss with Hayden was about far more than their lips meeting and an attraction they weren't aware of blooming. For Tate, it was about discovering that he'd been sleepwalking through his life.

Tate had never been ill-equipped for a task set before him. He'd accepted the gift of Spright Island from his father without qualms and had set about building an entire town and community even when he'd never worked on his own before. He'd learned by doing. Each time adversity had come up, he'd defeated it.

When he'd found out that Reid was his brother, Tate felt like a superhero who'd stumbled across his fatal weakness. He didn't have a single weapon in his arsenal to handle the situation set before him.

His previously drama-free life had begun to look more like a Netflix feature with him in the center as the hapless protagonist.

Until the kiss with Hayden.

That night had changed him, changed his outlook. And after a numb month of disbelief, feeling something— feeling anything other than stark shock—was as welcome as…well, as the kiss itself.

Yoga by Hayden came into sight and he crossed the street with a neat jog. A smile inched across his face, but flagged when he noticed the Closed sign on the door. He tugged the handle.

Locked.

He checked the clock on his phone. 12:04 p.m. He was late. Maybe she drew a hard line when it came to promptness.

Then he looked up and there she was, her curves barely contained in colorful leggings and a long-sleeved green shirt. She flipped the lock and opened the door, reminding him of the night he'd been standing outside this very studio in the rain.

Reminding him that she'd climbed to her toes to lay the mother of all kisses on him and had changed his life for the better.

"Sorry. Typically, I'm more punctual than this," she said.

God, he wanted to kiss her. The timing was wrong,

though. She hadn't yet met his eyes save for a brief flicker that bounced away the second she caught him staring.

She was hard not to stare at, all that silken dark hair and the grace in her every movement…

"I thought maybe you'd changed your mind." He hung his coat on a hook and perused a small display of yoga mats, blocks and water bottles. "I'll have to buy a mat. I don't have one."

"Help yourself." Hayden's gaze glanced off him again, and then almost relieved, she said, "Oh, good, she's here."

A fortysomething blonde woman ran toward the building, her yoga mat under her arm.

"Sherry had a last-minute need for an appointment, so I piggybacked onto your session. With the holiday week being so busy, I couldn't fit her in any other time." Hayden blew out the news in a nonstop stream. "I hope you don't mind."

Of course he minded. He'd scheduled a one-on-one with Hayden, and now he had to share his time with Sherry Baker, SWC's premiere real estate agent.

"Oh, hi, Tate." Sherry patted him on the shoulder before hanging her coat and scarf on the hook next to his. "I didn't know you practiced yoga."

He slid his eyes to Hayden, who bit her lip and locked the door. She'd double booked herself on purpose. *For some reason.*

"You know me," he told Sherry. "I'm always trying to support more local businesses."

"Get this one." Sherry handed him a black yoga mat. "It's manly and the same brand as mine."

"Done." He turned to Hayden with a million questions he couldn't ask. "Mind if I pay you after?"

Her mouth hovered open for a beat as Sherry unrolled her yoga mat. With an audience, Hayden didn't have much of a choice other than being polite.

"Sure."

"Great." He took his spot on the studio floor. He'd won that round. He planned on sticking around after Sherry left. He wanted answers.

Five

For Hayden, doing yoga was like breathing. She slipped into each pose easily, pausing to instruct Sherry and Tate through the movements.

Sherry was in her midforties with two teenagers. Her son had recently moved to a college campus and her younger daughter was thirteen and embroiled in a teenage spat with her two best friends, Callie and Samantha. Hayden knew this because Sherry hadn't stopped talking since class had started.

Sherry also mentioned her twenty unwanted pounds and a caffeine habit that bordered on addiction, and said she hoped doing one healthy thing like yoga would lead to other healthy things like cutting down on coffee and overtime at work.

Tate remained resolutely silent, though she'd caught

a small smile on his mouth more than once as he'd eased from one pose into the other.

During downward dog pose Hayden moved to assist Sherry with her alignment. "Push your five fingertips into the mat rather than the palm of your hand," she instructed. "We don't want compressed wrists."

Hayden turned to Tate next, willing herself to remember she was a teacher and a professional. There was never anything sexual involved in helping a student.

Until now.

One look at Tate's ass, his legs and arms strong and straight, and a wave of attraction walloped her in the stomach. As fate would have it, she was also going to have to touch his hips to move him into more of a V form than a U.

Dammit.

One hand on his back, the other on his hips, she instructed him to lower his heels to the floor as much as he was able. He breathed out with the effort, that breath reverberating along her arm and hand, and she became even more aware of him than before.

Who knew that was possible?

Those sorts of thoughts were exactly what Sherry's presence was supposed to *quell*.

She led them from downward dog to cobra, encouraging Sherry to use her knees if she needed to. When Hayden turned to tell Tate the same thing, he lowered into the pushup-like pose with what appeared to be very little effort. A closer look at his biceps and she realized they shook subtly as he took his time, holding himself in plank pose a moment before dropping his waist and pushing up with his arms.

She stared, unabashedly, which he must've noticed a moment later, when he sent her a cocky smirk.

Show-off.

She returned to her mat and walked them through one more sun salutation, ending in mountain pose: standing, hands in prayer pose at the chest.

"Namaste," Hayden said. "That concludes our lesson for the day."

"Woo! That was intense, girlfriend!" Sherry waved her hands in front of her pink face. "I'm sure Tate would've preferred a less chatty partner, though."

Sherry winked at him, and Hayden smothered a laugh. Sherry was happily married and treated Tate like she would a friend or any other familiar resident of SWC.

You know, the same way you *should be treating him.*

"I have to return to the office," Sherry announced. "Can I call to schedule a follow-up after the holiday?"

"Whenever you like." Hayden walked Sherry to the door, chatting to stall while waiting for Tate to leave. Instead, Tate was at the front desk, his rolled mat on the surface.

Crap. She forgot he needed to pay.

Sherry left and Hayden made her way to the front desk, her heart hammering.

"If you admit that you booked Sherry because you couldn't trust yourself to be alone with me, I'll forgive you for it," he told her.

"Ha!" She left it at that because any response other than "Yep, that's correct!" would have been a lie.

She *didn't* trust herself alone with him. His kiss the other night had been too welcome, his presence too distracting. She had enough drama in her life without creating some of her own.

Last night after he left she'd thought more about the chaos in Tate's life. Not one parental pair but two. And a surprise twin brother. Hayden had come to Spright Island specifically to avoid drama not become embroiled in it. That, and the fact she didn't trust herself to be alone with him, was why she'd scheduled Sherry for the same timeslot.

Tate wasn't unlike that second serving of ice cream she knew she shouldn't have. It seemed that no amount of willpower could keep her from one more taste.

"Thirty-two dollars."

He handed her his credit card.

"It's a really good mat," she explained needlessly as she charged his card. Anything to fill the dead air between them.

"I wasn't arguing."

"No, I guess you wouldn't." She imagined thirty-two dollars to Tate Duncan must be what thirty-two *cents* felt like to her.

"What's going on, Hayden? Do you find me particularly hard to get along with?"

"I— Sorry. That was rude." She handed his card back and flipped the screen around for him to sign it. When he was finished, she tucked her iPad into the drawer and, with no other task before her, was forced to meet his eyes.

He stood there like he had nowhere else to be.

"I didn't schedule Sherry *only* because I didn't want

to be alone with you. It worked well since you're both beginners."

He nodded slowly.

"Plus, what did you expect after you barged in here—"

"I barged?"

"—and demanded—"

"Demanded?"

She huffed out a breath. If was going to continue calling her bluff, she really should stop lying about her true intentions. But there was a nugget of truth she could cling to.

"My schedule has been nuts this week. Everyone's trying to get in before Thanksgiving."

"Ah. And you fit me in." He grinned. "Because you couldn't tell me no."

She made a pathetic choking sound. How arrogant was this guy, anyway? And how did he keep guessing right?

"Because I have to make a living. I don't have billions stashed away…" She almost added "like some people" but she was already protesting too much.

"Right," he agreed, but something in his expression told her he'd gleaned what she hadn't said. "Well, thank you. For the mat."

He went to grab his coat, slipping it over his arms and holding the rolled mat between his knees.

Feeling a dab of guilt, she moved toward him and vomited out a generic nicety. "Thank you for booking your session. I hope you'll consider a membership."

His hand resting on the door handle, he turned as she stopped advancing, putting her mere inches from his handsome face. "I was thinking about another kind of one-on-one session. Are you available for dinner?"

She hadn't been prepared for that. Words eluded her. She knew that agreeing to go out with him was a bad idea, but when faced with his glittering blue eyes she couldn't quite remember why.

"Just so you know—" that blue gaze dipped to her mouth "—if you were ready, I'd kiss the hell out of you right now. Just to make sure I didn't imagine how good you tasted before."

She gaped at him, but he didn't advance to kiss her. Instead he turned around and stepped outside.

Before she could shut the door, he pushed it open a crack. "Think about dinner. I'll ask again."

She locked up behind him, watching him through the glass. He had a sure, strong gait, a disgustingly handsome mug, and looked as good in a suit as he did in sweatpants.

There were a multitude of reactions fighting for first place. She wanted to open the door and yell for him to come back. She wanted to run upstairs and shut the blinds. She wanted to jog across the street and grab him by the ears and kiss the hell out of *him*.

Especially that last one.

While she warred with those options, frozen in stunned bliss at the possibilities, Tate grew farther and farther away until he was a shadowy blur disappearing into a path into the woods.

"Damn him." But she didn't mean it. She was looking forward to next time—when she would leave *him* slack-jawed and without a response.

Six

Chaz's Pub in Seattle was a far cry from the Brass Pony, with its scuffed floors and beaten tables. Tate walked in for the first time, took in the colorful red and green decorations, and decided he liked the place. Any establishment that decorated for Christmas before Thanksgiving had his undying respect.

His brother Reid had invited him out to celebrate "the biggest drinking day of the year," tacking on, "You're British and it's your duty to get pissed."

As overwhelming as it was to learn he had a brother and a set of parents he'd never met, Tate had to smile. Could've been the yoga. He'd been more relaxed since the session with Hayden, though the buzz afterwards could likely be blamed more on sexual tension than downward dog.

The sexual tension part wasn't entirely her fault.

Tate and Claire hadn't slept together since he'd found out about his family, and shortly after that she'd ended their engagement. In other words, it'd been a while.

Plus, Hayden was sexy as hell, had a way of revving him up and calming him down simultaneously. When she hadn't been touching him to move his body into proper form, he'd noticed her sliding from position to position. It'd been like watching an erotic dance.

She was a unique experience, that was for damn sure.

"Tate, hey!"

A petite brunette bounced over to him, pulling him from his thoughts. Reid's fiancée, Drew Fleming was as sweet as she was adorable and at the same time up to absolutely no good. He'd met her before—Reid had brought her when they'd gone out for drinks or dinners.

She looped her left arm in Tate's, and he glanced down at the sizable diamond ring on her hand. Reid had proposed around the time Tate's engagement had ended, as if Reid was an alien who had taken over Tate's life. Wasn't Tate supposed to be the one with the stable family life and fiancée?

"The boys are over there. I'll walk with you. But then I'm returning to the dance floor with the girls. Andy and Sabrina," she reminded him.

"Fiancées of Gage and Flynn."

"You remembered!"

He had. Gage and Flynn were Reid's best friends and coworkers. He'd met the whole gang in passing at one time or another.

Drew guided Tate to a high, round table with several stools surrounding it. Full glasses of Guinness were in front of each of the guys, suggesting they hadn't been here long.

"There he is." Reid wore the wide smile Tate envied. Not that Tate didn't want his brother to be happy, but he'd like to stockpile some of that for himself. Wanted to feel with certainty that tomorrow would come, and things would return to normal again.

"Found a stray," Drew released Tate and laid a kiss on Reid's cheek. He didn't let her get away, snagging her waist and dipping her low while kissing her thoroughly. Next to them, Flynn grinned, but Gage was less enthralled by the PDA.

"Still getting used to that," Gage grumbled as Tate took his seat. Gage was Drew's older brother, and Reid and Drew had kept their relationship from Gage until long after things had gotten serious between them.

"Hang in there, buddy." Flynn slapped Gage's back and let out a baritone chuckle. "Tate, man, how are you?"

Tate nodded, having no other word than a generic "fine."

"You need a beer," Flynn announced, waving down a waitress and to order one.

"Off with you, then." Reid swatted his fiancée's butt and she giggled, radiantly aglow. Once she'd scampered off, Reid's smile stuck to his face like glue. "She's pregnant."

Flynn nearly spit out his beer.

Gage turned an interesting shade of pale green.

"Congratulations," Tate said, figuring that was a safe response given the size of Reid's grin.

"Are pigs flying?" Flynn asked, his eyebrows meeting over the bridge of his nose. "Did hell freeze over? Am I having a stroke?" He turned to Gage and asked, "Do you smell burned toast?"

Gage shook his head, but his color returned. "Maybe we're all suffering from strokes. Reid Singleton: engaged and soon-to-be dad. What gives?"

"Drew. She's...Drew." Reid grinned bigger.

"I know how amazing she is. She's *my* sister." Then, as if it dawned on him at that moment, Gage smiled, too. "I'm going to be an uncle."

"Me, too. Technically." Flynn shrugged.

"And you," Reid dipped his chin at Tate. "Legitimately."

Right. Tate hadn't thought about that. Reid wasn't only a friend he was getting to know. He was a blood relative. The waitress delivered a Guinness, and Tate drank down the top third without coming up for air.

A pair of high-pitched squeals lifted on the air, and the guys turned toward the dance floor, where a brunette with glasses and a tall redhead were hugging Drew simultaneously.

"She told 'em. I knew she couldn't hold out." Reid said that with a smile as well, and if Tate had to guess, he'd say his brother's joy wasn't going anywhere soon.

"Sláinte." Flynn held his glass aloft, and the four of them banged the beers together. "So what have you been up to with the wellness commune, Duncan?"

He'd only met Flynn twice, but had determined that joking was Flynn's style. Tate liked Reid's friends and their fiancées. They were good people.

"Planning on a big Thanksgiving dinner Friday for

the residents," Tate answered. "Serving Kool-Aid at the end for the really dedicated."

The guys laughed at the cult reference. Tate took it as a win. He knew the way Spright Wellness Community had been perceived it the past, but the place had gained a reputation for luxury living, thanks to Tate. Visitors flocked to the island and filled their community to capacity to eat, shop or simply spend time in nature.

"What about you guys?" Tate asked.

"Family dinner." Reid slid a glance at Gage. "With that wanker."

"I tried to disinvite him, but Mom said it'd ruin the holiday," Gage returned, poker-faced.

"We're going to California to Sab's parents. Her brother, Luke, is flying in from Chicago to join us."

"He's in Chi-town now?" Reid asked. "Sabrina never told me that."

"Yeah. His new gym franchise took off and he moved there to open another one. Rumor has it he's bringing a girl. Another one bites the dust." Flynn hadn't kept it a secret that his family was no longer. He'd mentioned inheriting Monarch Consulting after his father had died. That had brought mention of his late mother followed by a tasteless joke about how his brother was "banging my ex-wife." Flynn didn't seem as bitter about it as he was matter-of-fact, which Tate respected. Here he was trying to handle one curveball, and Flynn had been swinging at them his entire adult life.

"What about you?" Reid asked. "Other than Friday. Any plans?"

"Uh, no. Not really. Couldn't make the trip to Cali to see the parents."

Reid nodded slowly, like there was a thought he didn't want to say aloud in front of the guys. Like maybe he'd figured out that Tate couldn't handle a family holiday with his adoptive parents after finding out they'd basically bought him off the black market. They hadn't known the truth, though, and that was the only reason he was still speaking to them. "The Brass Pony is serving an eight-course dinner. I thought about going."

"You're welcome to join us," Gage said, even as Tate held up a hand to tell him he didn't have to do that. "I'm not asking because you're a charity case. I'm asking because you're Reid's brother. Plus my parents cook enough to feed the county."

As kind as the invite was, a holiday spent with a family he didn't know and as the only single guy at the table sounded like Tate's worst nightmare. Rather than say that, he covered with, "Actually, I have a friend who lives in town. I asked her to join me."

Technically he hadn't asked Hayden out for that specific night but the dinner invitation could have been for whenever, wherever.

"You *dog*. Dating again already?" Reid smirked.

"Claire and I weren't..." Tate took in the three girls who belonged with the men at the table as he tried to decide how to finish that sentence. For lack of a better term, he landed on, "Like you and your girls."

"Enviably gorgeous?" Reid said.

"In love," Tate said, bringing the table's laughter to a halt.

"Damn." Flynn finished his beer and gestured for another round for the table. Tate took another hearty gulp to catch up, but he still wasn't close. "Duncan called us out."

"He does that," Reid said.

"I like him," Gage decided. "Even if he doesn't want to hang out with my loony family on turkey day."

The guys continued bantering, and Tate, for a change, found himself relaxing into the conversation, the beer and the round of appetizers they ended up ordering. He didn't feel like the odd man out with the girls back at the table, tittering about Drew's pregnancy and making sure she had first dibs on every appetizer plate, but it did make him think of Hayden and how well she would've fit in here.

It was time to extend that dinner invitation again. And this time, earn a yes.

Seven

Hayden, sitting at a table in Succulence, a trendy, gourmet vegetarian restaurant in SWC, waved her friends over. Arlene gave an exuberant wave and pulled Emily in alongside her.

Hayden had met Arlene and Em last year, and they'd become fast friends. In SWC, residents were more interested in what they had in common rather than what set them apart. It made for deep discussions early on and, had cemented the three of them.

Well, originally there had been four. But Bailey had been AWOL since having a baby. Joyously married, she'd always been in a category of her own. Hayden recalled many, many nights when she and Arlene and Em would complain about their recent bad date or #singlelife and Bailey didn't have anything to contribute. Hayden missed her, but was confident Bailey would fold back into the fray. They were too close for their friendship to end over a few lifestyle differences. Besides, one of the three of them was bound to be married or at least happily coupled off eventually…right?

"Girls' night is on!" Arlene, boisterous and bold, had so much confidence it was infectious. She was also hilarious. More often than not she had Hayden clutching her side in laughter while tears streamed down her face.

"So good to see you!" Emily gave Hayden a tight squeeze. "I feel like I've been gone a year." Emily had recently gone on an excursion to Spain for the lifestyle blog she wrote.

"It felt that way for all of us," Hayden agreed.

"Except we remembered you and you forgot all about us." Arlene threw her purse onto the chair. "First round on me. What's your pleasure? And before you ask, we're doing a shot followed by a cocktail. That's the minimum."

"Uh…" Hayden wasn't exactly a shot kind of girl. Not anymore.

"It ain't like any of us drove here." Arlene's blond hair was big with a lot of volume, like the rest of her. "And it *is* the biggest drinking holiday of the year."

"Because everyone dreads going home to family," Emily supplied. "Peppermint schnapps followed by a cosmo."

"I like your style." Arlene raised her brows at Hayden.

"Well…"

"Tequila," Arlene decided.

"What? No!" Hayden laughed.

"Yes. You can follow it with a light beer."

"I'll have a white Russian." Hayden lifted an eyebrow.

"Vodka shot on the side, then." Arlene didn't wait for an argument, only zoomed over to the bar to place their orders.

"Will you hold my hair?" Emily asked with a bright smile. She was ridiculously adorable with her dark hair in a sassy pixie cut. She folded her arms on the tabletop—white frosted glass balanced on a single silver pedestal. Succulence's mod design resembled a health spa, with its white and silver and neon-green accents. They were also pricey, but Hayden gladly overpaid for the fantastic food and cocktails.

A waiter came by. "Ladies."

"Hi, Josh." Em smiled up at him, as smitten as she was the first time they'd come in here. Hayden took pride in the fact that she'd arrived early enough to request his table.

"Eating or drinking tonight?" Josh was probably five years younger than all of them, but damned if Emily cared. She leaned heavily on a palm.

"Drinking, but snacks later. We'll probably camp here a while, but I promise to leave you a pile of money for a tip."

"Your beauty is enough of a tip for me." His cunning smile scrunched his dark eyes up at the corners. Paired with his tanned complexion and dark hair, Hayden had to agree he was pretty darn cute.

"You are full of it," Arlene told him as she returned to the table, tray in hand.

"Give me that." Josh swiped the tray and pointed at a seat. Arlene obediently sat and let Josh serve their drinks. "I know the peppermint schnapps is Em's."

Emily batted her lashes.

"Arlene has to be the tequila. And Hayden—" he sniffed her clear shot "—vodka. Nice choice. Enjoy, ladies." Then he was off, but not before winking at Emily.

"Oh, will you two screw each other already?" Arlene drank down a healthy swallow of her margarita .

"Shh! These walls have ears. And eyes. And cell phones with cameras." Emily jerked her gaze around the room.

Emily was right. SWC was high-end, luxurious and nature- and wellness-focused, but it was also a dressed-up small town. Everyone knew everyone and therefore knew everyone's *business*.

"We should've gone to the city where we could gossip properly," Arlene said. "Shots, ladies."

"If we were in the city, then I couldn't request Josh as a server and watch Emily light up like a Christmas tree," Hayden said.

"I do not!" Emily turned a stunning shade of red as she lifted her shot glass.

"Did you think it was coincidence that we're always at his table?" Arlene asked with a raspy chuckle.

"You should ask him out," Hayden said.

"No way. He's just patronizing me."

"He'd like to be doing more than that." Arlene slanted a glance at Hayden.

"Why don't *you* ask someone out?" Em shot back, her shot wobbling at the edge of the glass. "How long's it been since you dated Derek?"

"Not long enough." Arlene held her shot aloft and shouted, "Cheers to years of beers and pap smears!"

Emily turned bright pink, Hayden groaned and hid behind a hand, and Arlene let out a bawdy laugh. That broad. God. Hayden loved her, though. They chucked back their shots, only Em coughing and waving the air like she'd swallowed gasoline.

"What about you, Hayd?" Em croaked.

"What about me what?"

"When are you going to ask someone out?"

"Why would I ask someone out?" Hayden purposely widened her eyes to look more innocent and then tacked on, "When I can kiss…" She looked around the restaurant teeming with their neighbors. Everyone here knew or had at least heard of Tate Duncan, so she couldn't very well blurt out his name. "*Someone* any time I'd like," she finished with an arch of one eyebrow.

"Shut. Up." Emily leaned in. "Who?"

"Someone we know." Arlene assessed Hayden. "But who?"

Unable to resist, Hayden mouthed his name. "Tate."

"Duncan?" Arlene bleated.

"Shh!" Hayden hissed.

"See? It's not fun when she does it to *you*." Em stuck her tongue out at Arlene, who returned the sentiment.

"He was standing outside my studio in the rain one night, and he looked so lost. I invited him up for tea and then…"

"You had sex with him?" Arlene cried.

"Keep it down, and no, I didn't!"

"Why not?" Emily asked with a small pout.

"For the same reason you won't ask out Josh," Hayden answered. "I was too terrified to consider it."

Which was the truth, if not for different reasons than Em. Hayden had fought hard to be fiercely independent, to escape the chaos that bubbled over in her family on a daily basis. Tate wasn't exactly a complete set. Some of his parts were scattered across the damn globe.

"I heard he and the blonde split up," Arlene said.

"Where did you hear that?"

"Naomi. She was at the café and overheard them talking."

Damn. This place really was a gossip mill. Hayden didn't dare mention Tate's learning of his birth parents and a twin brother.

"So, I'd be rebound girl," Hayden said, and it wasn't an entirely bad setup. Seeing how mired her mother was with her father certainly hadn't made it look appealing.

"Sounds like a superhero," Em said. "Rebound Girl! Able to leap tall, handsome billionaires in a single bound."

"I don't think he's a *billionaire*," Hayden said through her laughter.

"Have you seen this place?" Arlene gestured beyond the restaurant to the rows of houses on one side and the retail establishments on the other. "He built it, Hayd. From scratch."

"I have nothing against wealthy men," Emily said. "Except I'm attracted to the ones who aren't." She sent another longing glance to Josh, who was jotting down another group's order.

"He doesn't count, since he owns Succulence. He could be a billionaire restaurant owner. You never know," Hayden supplied.

Em pursed her lips in consideration.

"Well, I wouldn't kick Tate Duncan out of bed for any reason. *Especially* if it was because he was loaded." Arlene waggled her eyebrows, Emily agreed and Hayden found herself easing into the conversation as her mind wandered along the path of what-if and arrived at Tate's bed.

And Tate's couch. And Tate's shower…

"You're thinking about sex!" Arlene said. "Josh! We need another round!"

"No, we don't." But Hayden's smile was too big to be denied. She *was* thinking about sex. Tate was too fun not to kiss, not to do a host of other things to, especially since his last words to her were about kissing the hell out of her when she was ready. "I don't know if I'm ready."

Then again…

Just because Hayden wanted to have an affair with a gorgeous rich guy didn't mean she had to give up her autonomy. Tate didn't *have* to be ice cream. He could be a perfectly reasonable kale salad, which she enjoyed immensely and never suffered cravings for afterwards.

Aw, who was she kidding? Tate could never be kale salad. He was too tempting. Too hot. Too distracting!

But she should give herself more credit. She was independent. She'd moved away from her family and started over with her new family: her friends at SWC. She was a successful business owner, to boot.

Plus she really, *really* wanted to say yes to Tate the next time he asked. For dinner, for a kiss, for anything…

"On second thought, I *could be* ready." Hayden stirred the cream into her dark drink.

"Attagirl." Arlene pinned Emily with a meaningful look. "Now are you going to ask out Josh, or do I have to do it for you?"

Eight

Laughing, the three ladies stumbled out of Succulence and onto the sidewalk.

Arlene curled her arm around Emily and let out a shout of triumph. "You freaking did it!"

Emily giggled, proud of herself. She should be. After round two of drinks, she'd looked up at Josh and purred, "We should go on a date sometime. My friends agree we'd look good together."

To Hayden's complete delight, Josh's lids had lowered sexily and he'd replied, "What took you so long to ask?"

"Don't get too excited." Emily belted her coat against the wind. "It's only the beginning. And beginnings are fragile."

"You mean the other F-word," Arlene said. "Fun."

"They are fun," Emily agreed.

"Well, I had a fantastic time. Goodnight, loves." Hayden kissed Emily's cheek and pulled Arlene into a hug. "Be safe!"

They'd eaten enough appetizers to soak up the alcohol and had switched to water after the drinks. Two hours of fun and laughter later, Hayden's heart was full and happy. Her walk home might not be warm, but it would be welcome. Moving her body always made her feel better.

Back home in Seattle, Hayden used to hang out with the wrong crowd. She used to drink not for recreation, but with the goal of being completely drunk. She used to wake up with hangovers and headaches and, one time, no memory of how she'd gotten home. Nothing was more sobering than realizing she was repeating a pattern that her grandmother had started. Worried that she might end up exactly like Grandma Winnie, a belligerent, controlling, bitter alcoholic, Hayden decided that maybe drinking shouldn't be her main focus in life.

Enter exercise. She'd started with running early in the morning, which kept her from staying up too late. Running didn't require special equipment or training, and she found she had a proclivity for it. She set goals to be better each week and before she knew it, she was running every day.

Bitten by the fitness bug, she left her sedentary office job, where her derriere was widening by the day, to work at a local gym. She took advantage of her employee discount to purchase yoga classes.

It was love at first warrior pose.

Yoga gave her something running didn't. *Peace.*

Rather than her heart rate ratcheting up and her

feet pounding the pavement—it was hell on her knees, anyway—she spent each hour-long yoga class in an almost meditative state. Working quietly and silently on moving her body and stretching stubborn muscles.

Yoga had been the first domino to fall in her quest for self-care. She wanted to be good to herself rather than continue the abuse she'd started in her twenties. Yoga led her to Spright Island. Yoga awakened her to the unhealthy relationship she had with her family. Yoga made her want to be better *for herself.*

At her studio, she rounded the corner to enter the side door that led up to her apartment. She should hang lights this year. Every year she balked at hanging outdoor holiday lights, seeing it as a hassle and dreading taking them down after the season was over. But maybe it was time to stretch another muscle and step beyond her comfort zone. Besides, it would be worth it to see them and smile, knowing she cared enough to adorn her little porch with Christmas cheer.

Doorknob in hand, she didn't make it inside before friendly honk sounded. A white Mercedes with tinted windows pulled to her side of the street, the car belonging to the man who wouldn't leave her mind.

Tate stepped out and rounded the car, his hands in the pockets of his leather jacket. His long legs were encased in denim, ending in leather slip-ons. Even several yards away he was tempting and potent.

Totally more like ice cream than kale salad.

"I'm not stalking you, I swear." He grinned, and damned if she couldn't help returning it. "I was thinking of you tonight."

She'd been thinking of him, too, but couldn't quite bring herself to admit it.

"Can I buy you a drink? A meal?"

"I was just out with friends. I'm fed, and I've had all the drinks I'm having for one night." Tonight had been a little over-the-top for her. She rarely indulged, for obvious reasons.

Tate fell silent and Hayden wondered she was playing too hard to get. Before she could worry she'd thwarted his efforts entirely, he asked, "Can I show you my place?"

Her teeth stabbed her lip, her smile struggling to stay restrained. Emily had mentioned beginnings and how fragile they were while Arlene had argued that they were fun. Given Hayden's thundering pulse and warmth pooling in her belly, she'd have to agree with Arlene.

"Okay."

He closed the distance between them and held out a hand. Hayden slipped her palm into his. With each step, she was reassured she'd made the right decision. She'd had an amazing night already. Capping it off with a visit to Tate's house that would lead to whatever they pleased was the ultimate way to end it.

"You keep getting hotter." He shook his head as if awed.

"Yeah, well, so do you."

They stood in the street and grinned at each other like idiots for a beat, and then he helped her into the car.

When he pulled away from the curb her belly tightened in anticipation. It had been a long while since she'd felt wanted. A few years since she'd attempted to have a relationship. Her last boyfriend, Alan, had been good for her at the time. He was stable, nice and had a great job. But the more time she spent with him the less like herself she'd felt. He enjoyed staying in so she found herself staying in more. He didn't like seafood and she realized at one point that she hadn't cooked her favorite shrimp pasta in months. She'd lost herself in him, and again those old patterns she'd seen in her family became apparent. After Alan, she decided to make sure she never lost herself again.

Which made her briefly question how hard she'd fought Tate's advances. She'd resisted him in the name of maintaining her independence. Now that they were in his Mercedes gliding along the tree-lined streets, she had to question her reasoning. What could be more pro-self than indulging in the attraction pounding between them?

"I was thinking about you tonight, too," she said. She was done resisting.

His face was lit by the blue dashboard lights of his car, his grin one for the books.

He cut through Summer's Drift, one of her favorite neighborhoods in SWC. The theme was water, the palette white and sand and pale blues. Residents took the theme to heart and decorated accordingly. There were coils of rope resting on porches and miniature lighthouses standing in yards. One house even had upstairs windows that resembled ship's portals.

"Where'd you have dinner?" Tate asked.

"Succulence."

"Best sweet potato gnocchi in town."

"Not afraid of veggie fare?"

"Would a guy who built this community fear vegetables?" he joked.

"Fair point. What about you?"

"I was out with my brother. A bar called Chaz's Pub in Seattle."

"Chaz. One of the lesser-known Irishmen. How was it?"

"Good. Really good." He didn't say more but he didn't have to. She could tell by his tone and the quiet way he finished their trip that he'd had a "really good" evening. She was glad to hear he was getting along well with his newfound brother.

He turned down a long drive hooded by trees and marked by a private sign. Hayden was excited to see Tate's house. She'd always been curious what kind of house the builder of Spright Wellness Community had built for himself.

The trees ended and the house came into view. The structure was boxy but interesting thanks to the slanted roof that lent a modern, artistic quality to the home. It was big, but not as big as she was expecting. Arlene's billionaire reference had Hayden expecting an over-the-top fifty-room mansion.

"It's beautiful," she commented as he pulled into a driveway.

In the light glowing from the porch and the car's headlights she could make out the details. A sturdy stone wall climbed to the top of the house, while the rest of it was dark metal beams and wood. At the highest point of the roof, one entire side was almost nothing but windows, intersected with a set of stairs that led to an outdoor patio.

"Wait till you see the inside." He unbuckled her belt for her and they climbed out of the car.

"Living room through here." He gestured as they walked into the foyer, pausing to shrug out of his leather coat. "Kitchen's to your right. Can I take your coat?"

"Sure." Big hands moved to her shoulders. Flanked by his heat from behind, it took everything in her not to lean into his warmth.

He slipped the garment from her shoulders, leaning close to her ear to mutter, "Better?"

A tight breath was all she could manage.

She walked through the living room and admired the décor. Metal and wood and stone converged in a modern, artistic, comfortable way. Everywhere she looked, there was nature. From the petrified wood on a stand on the bookshelf to the woven rug beneath the black leather sofa and chairs.

"Mind if I powder my nose?" she asked when Tate walked into the room with her.

He pointed to the slatted-step staircase framed with an iron railing. "Top of the stairs. Take a right. Can I get you anything to drink?"

"Sparkling water? Or still, if that's too fussy."

"Lucky you. We specialize in fussy here."

In the bathroom mirror she fluffed her hair and gave herself a once-over. She looked good tonight. Thank goodness she'd worn her favorite low-heeled boots. They made her ass look amazing.

Tate had turned on music. She heard the croony voice of Michael Bublé drifting through the downstairs. Curious to see the rest of the house, she peeked down the hallway on one side and then the other. Admittedly she was being nosy, but she couldn't help it. She'd always been epically curious about how the other half lived.

At best guess Tate had spared no expense when it came to decorating and furnishing his house.

There were four bedrooms upstairs alone, and still more house to explore downstairs. One of the rooms was being used as an office, the tidy space both masculine and attractive. The enormous L-shaped desk was deep brown in color, the desk chair the same pale beige as the reading chair in the corner. A laptop was centered on the desk's surface, a square pen holder holding three pens next to it. Bookshelves lined the wall stuffed with an array of architectural books and business titles.

She bypassed a guest room, and another being used for storage. A box marked "Claire" sat on the floor, and she peeked inside. A white sweater and pair of oversize headphones were all she'd evidently left behind.

The last bedroom at the end of the hall held a model of a neighborhood in the center of a large folding table. The model had several buildings, including apartments and what looked like a retail area, as well as a a green slab with tiny benches and a swing set.

"You found my secret project," said a voice behind her.

"Oh!" Startled, she straightened quickly and bumped the table. She turned just as quickly to steady the model, grateful she didn't knock it off and turn the impressive work of art into a pile of matchsticks.

"Sorry. I'm sorry." She backed away from the table. "I was… Um. I like how you decorate. Your house is amazing."

"Relax, Hayden. I don't think you were casing my house in search of the good silver." He handed her a champagne flute. "Your sparkling water. I added a wedge of lime. I do well with fussy."

She hummed, keeping her thoughts about Claire to herself.

"Is it really secret?" she asked of the model.

"No, but very few people know about it. This neighborhood is going to sit behind Summer's Drift. We're building around the trees. The architecture is Swedish. Row houses, a few restaurants." He pointed out the various elements.

"And a park."

"And a park." He assessed her, eyes narrowed.

"What?"

"It's just—"

"What is it?" She straightened her sweater and reached for her hair, fidgeting.

"You look ready now, Hayden Green."

Oh.

Oh.

"To have the hell kissed out of me?" she guessed.

He set her glass aside, his gaze zooming in on her mouth. "I'm guessing that's going to require a lot of kissing."

She rested her arms on his shoulders. "Are you up for the task?"

"Hell, *yes*," he said, his voice gravel. And then he smothered her laughter with a rough kiss.

Nine

Kissing Hayden was like being kissed for the first time.

He moved his lips over hers, a unique thrill jolting him as she gripped the back of his head and dove in for more. Her tongue came out to play, nudging his top lip before her teeth nipped his bottom lip.

No, screw that. Kissing Hayden was like being kissed *by Hayden* for the first time. If he'd been kissed like this for his first kiss, he would've had no idea what to do next.

Thank God he knew now.

Opening to accept her tongue, he deepened the kiss, wrapping his arms around her lower back and pressing her soft body against his. She was fit, muscular and curvy, but there was give where there should be. In her breasts flattening against his chest, and her belly, which made for a perfect place to nudge the hint of his erection.

Kissing Claire was never like this.

He shouldn't compare, but he couldn't keep from doing it. Couldn't keep from noticing that Hayden's strength and softness were two attributes that his ex had never had. Claire was controlled, buttoned-up. Tate had mirrored those attributes, which made for some uninspired sex.

He couldn't think of a scenario where *Hayden* and *uninspired* would go together in a sentence.

"I promised myself," she whispered, tugging his hair, "the next chance I had—" she stole a quick kiss "—I'd do this."

"Kiss me?" he asked before she lit him up with another tongue lashing.

She pulled her lips away and regarded him with disbelief. "Have sex with you."

"You want to have sex with me?" he growled.

She rolled her eyes. "Oh, like you don't want to have sex with me?"

Her confidence was his favorite part about her. The second was her body. He gripped her hips and squeezed, loving the contrasting strength and give there, as well. "I do. I really, *really* do."

Something serious shadowed her eyes. The tugging she'd done earlier to his hair changing to gentle strokes. She tipped her chin and took him in, her dark eyes both earnest and vulnerable.

Leaning in slowly, he gave her the chance to change her mind, to back away and thank him for the invite and insist he drive her home. He would. He didn't want to, but he would.

She instead closed the gap between them, her lips barely brushing his as she gave him room to initiate.

Hell. Yes.

He wouldn't miss the chance to sleep with her tonight. Not when she tasted and felt this good—and he sensed she needed the physical connection as badly as he did.

Threading her hair through his fingers, he took charge of her mouth. He bent his knees to lower them to the floor and she followed, easing down with him in one fluid, graceful movement. He took a mental snapshot of her on his carpeted floor, her hair spread around her like a dark halo. She was gorgeous and, for now, *his*.

He braced his weight on his arms and hovered over her, studying her unique beauty. Until her lips spread into an uncertain smirk. "You're staring again."

"Can't help it."

"Why? Is there a problem?"

"Holding out longer than ten minutes, maybe."

"Well, forget it then." She winked, saucy, which only made him harder.

"I was admiring you. And wondering how I missed that you were this exquisite until the night you found me loitering outside your studio in the driving rain."

She stroked his hair gently. "I was admiring you that night, too."

"I was kidding about the ten minutes. Let's make this last." He covered her mouth with his own, and she returned his efforts. While her fingernails tickled his scalp, he skimmed his hand along her sweater, lifting it until he encountered a slice of soft skin. A low groan reverberated from his chest, and he reminded himself that he'd promised to make this last. As badly as he wanted her naked, he was going to take his time. He had one shot at convincing her to sleep with him more than once. After that first kiss she'd so boldly initiated, he knew *once* would not be enough.

He had to impress her.

He rucked her shirt up and exposed her taut abdomen—delicately defined, he could make out the muscles above her belly button. There was softness to the bit below, and he again admired the juxtaposition. Beauty wasn't found in the expected, but in the surprises; the imperfect.

He moved down her body to kiss her stomach and then back up to her bra. Gold and black and lace held breasts that were large and round. He was definitely going to need a moment with each of them. He helped her sit up and divested her of her sweater. Hayden shivered.

"Cold?" he asked.

"Excited," she answered. He loved her honesty.

"Flattery, Ms. Green, will get you absolutely *everywhere*."

"Sucker," she whispered.

Smacking a brief kiss onto the center of her cunning mouth, he found the hook of her bra, failed at releasing it and tried again.

"Out of practice?" She reached behind her to unhook it herself.

"Yeah. I guess I am." It'd been a while since he'd

undressed Claire. He realized with stark discomfort that they'd usually undressed themselves before sex. What a waste. This was the best part.

Bra loosened, Hayden slipped it from her arms, watching his reaction as she exposed her breasts to the cooler air in the room.

Dusky rose, her nipples pebbled. He took one into his mouth and sucked gently. She reacted like he'd plugged her into an electric socket, zapping to life with an encouraging gasp as she raked her hands into his hair again.

He swirled the tender bud and then dragged his tongue over the other nipple and started on that one. She squirmed beneath him, lifting her hips to bump his. He was hard and well past ready but unwilling to rush—or so he had to keep reminding himself.

After she'd thoroughly wrecked his hair, he abandoned her breasts to undo her belt and unbutton her jeans. Halfway through unzipping, she reached for his sweater and yanked.

"Take this off."

It wasn't hard to take orders from a rosy-cheeked, topless woman on her back. Not even a little.

He whipped off the shirt and she ran her fingertips over his pectorals and stomach, and then along the line of hair that vanished into his jeans. She bypassed the belt and zipper and molded her hand around the stiff denim hiding his cock. If he thought he was hard before, that was nothing compared to the inches of steel created by her tenderly stroking hand.

Moving her wrist, he reprimanded her with a headshake and yanked her pants from her legs. He had her short boots to contend with, so that took a second or two of struggle.

Her black and gold panties made it worth the work.

"Tell me you always wear lingerie."

"I always wear lingerie."

"Even under your yoga pants?"

"I don't wear anything under my yoga pants."

Great. He could never take a class from her again without embarrassing himself.

"Your face." She chuckled, returning her hands to his abs. "Where have you been hiding this body? I guess I wasn't looking hard enough."

"Neither of us were." He kissed her palm and pulled the sides of her panties down her thighs as he laid kisses on her belly and thighs. Once he'd stripped them from her, he lifted one of her legs and rested it on his shoulder, enjoying the way she propped herself up to watch. She opened wider to accommodate him, not the least bit shy about accepting what she wanted.

And he wasn't the least bit shy about giving it to her.

It'd been so long since a man's mouth had been between her legs she was almost too excited to concentrate. *Almost.*

Tate worked his magic until she was forced to close her eyes, lie back and give herself over to his ministrations. He paid careful attention to what she liked, doubling his efforts whenever she let out a whimper of approval.

Which she did *a lot.*

The man had skills. She had the stray thought that she'd never dump a guy who could make her come as easily as Tate Duncan. That alone would be worth the price of admission.

A gentle series of orgasms hit her like rolling waves. Arching her back, she parted her thighs. He gripped her hips and tugged her toward his mouth, continuing his delicious assault until she was moaning again. There was another orgasm waiting on the cusp. She could feel it. She reached up to tug her own nipples, and that was exactly the move that took her over. Like one of those earlier waves, she came on a cry, undulating as pleasure rocked her body and erased her mind.

Her breath sawed from her lungs, leaving her body warm and buzzing. A shadow darkened her vision behind her eyelids.

"Open your eyes, beautiful girl," Tate murmured before kissing the corner of her mouth.

She was confronted with a tender ocean-blue stare.

"Hi," he said.

"Hi." She laughed at the absurdity of the greeting, at the sheer delight of it. She'd never had this much fun having sex, and technically they hadn't had sex yet.

"Condoms are in the bathroom across the hall," he told her. "Which means I have to leave the cradle of your incredible thighs, find one and come back."

"Okay." She nodded quickly to let him know she wasn't suffering an ounce of doubt where making love to him was concerned. She was all for it.

"Okay." He stood and stepped over her, adjusting the hard ridge pushing the fly of his jeans to capacity, and then walked into the hallway.

Hayden slapped her hands over her face and smiled

into her palms. She was really doing this. And it was *really* freaking incredible.

Tate returned in record time and, holding the condom wrapper between his teeth, wrestled free from his belt and jeans. She simply lay there and watched as he stripped for her, admiring the strong planes of his muscular body and the strength he exuded.

When he tugged off black boxer briefs, she felt her mouth go very dry. It was…well, it was gorgeous, was what it was. Long and thick and inviting, all brought to stark attention as he rolled the protection over his length.

"Keep looking at me like that, and we'll be done sooner than you'd like," he warned, lowering over her willing body.

"I don't believe you." She hooked her heels over his ass and tugged him forward, his heated skin warming hers. The hardness between his legs met her plush, wet folds and she gasped.

"You're far too capable, Tate Duncan—" she paused as he notched her entrance "—to finish before you're good and ready."

A feral, cocky glint lit his eyes as he seated himself deep inside her. Her mind blanked of thought as moved, slipping along the wetness he'd created with his talented mouth.

Hayden stopped teasing him and gave in to the pleasure he doled out blow by exquisite blow.

Ten

"Mmm." Hayden hummed, pure satisfaction.

Tate smiled over at the dark-haired beauty on the floor next to him, proud of those three letters making up one truncated sound. He'd worked hard.

"We're good at that," he stated.

"We are." Her throat bobbed with a husky, sexy laugh She turned her head to face him, and he was struck momentarily speechless by the unwavering eye contact. "I had complete faith in you."

Goose bumps prickled her arms and she shivered. He rolled to the side and rubbed her biceps with his hand in an attempt to warm her.

"How about some hot cocoa or tea?"

"I'd never turn down cocoa. Do you have marshmallows?"

"What am I, a barbarian? I have *homemade* marsh-mallows from Blossom Bakery."

"I love those." Her expression was a lot like her last O face, which made him grin.

He offered a hand and helped her sit up.

"Wow. I'm zapped." She put a hand to her hair. "I must be a mess."

"You are a mess. A complete and utter, distracting, hot mess."

"That…was a compliment, I assume?" She narrowed one eye.

"Yes." He kissed her succinctly. "What time are you going to Thanksgiving dinner tomorrow?" He knew some families ate earlier in the day—hell, his own mother set the table at 11:00 a.m.

"I'm—" She shook her head in a rare show of discomfort. "I'm not going anywhere for Thanksgiving. My family…we're sort of distant." The arms she'd wrapped around herself tightened.

"If you don't have anywhere to be in the morning then you should stay the night here."

"You want me to stay?"

"I do. Yes. And then I want to do what we just did three or four more times."

"Four!" she said on a laugh. "Four times before tomorrow morning?"

"Preferably."

He'd hardly know himself right now if he were an outside observer. He was beyond what should be comfortable with Hayden this soon.

After he'd learned of his actual birth parents and twin brother, Tate had vowed to deal with it like he had any other moment of adversity. Just plow through with certainty and confidence that it would work out in the end. He'd underestimated the emotional toll of finding out his entire existence was a lie.

His relationship with his adoptive parents had become strained—a totally new dynamic for them—and then Claire had ended the engagement. Tate began thinking that closeness wasn't something he was meant to have on a long-term basis.

He was having trouble categorizing Hayden, though. He liked being close to her. He liked her honesty and wit. He just plain liked her. Way more than he should.

Tate had played safe his entire life. Had laid out each step after the last in a predictable, cautious way. What good had playing it safe done him? He'd lost everything unexpectedly.

A part of him argued that he should be smart about this thing with Hayden—that he shouldn't get in too deep—and in response he raised a middle finger. He was trying a new tack. He was embracing danger and unpredictability for a change.

He needed to shake off the caution from his past. Needed to feel *alive*. And since no one made him feel more alive than Hayden Green, he needed *her*.

They both dressed, pausing to send satisfied smiles over at each other in between zipping and buckling. She tugged on her boots and pulled a hair tie from her pocket. In two seconds, and barely trying, she'd fashioned a ponytail.

"Impressive." Everything about her.

He took her hand and walked with her downstairs. Five minutes later he served her at his kitchen table,

setting a mug piled high with sticky, square marsh-
mallows in front of her.

She cradled the mug before navigating a sip of the
cocoa around the melting marshmallows. "Mmm."

"When you made that sound earlier, I liked it then,
too."

"Yes, well, you earned it."

Confidence straightened his shoulders at the comment and again when she looked around the room. He
admired it with her—the stylish gas fireplace, the wide
open windows with nothing but dark woods beyond.
His carefully chosen furnishings, earthy in both ma-
terials and color.

"I'd love to have this much space." She tilted her
head back to admire the overhead lighting. "Not that
I don't love living above my studio. But this…" She let
out a wistful sigh. "This is beautiful."

"Does that mean you're staying?"

"I didn't bring any clothes." She pressed a finger to
his lips when he opened his mouth to argue. "You're
going to say I don't need them."

"Damn straight." Movement outside caught his attention and he pulled her finger from his lips. "Look."

A deer poked its head from the trees, cocking its
ears to listen. Hayden let out a soft gasp of surprise.

"This is why I tucked my house into the woods. So?
You staying?"

"You think a deer is enough to get me to agree?"

"I was hoping that and the promise of sex four more
times before morning might seal the deal."

She chuckled, but didn't answer him.

"Tell me about your twin brother." She lifted her mug.

"Not the smoothest segue."

"Go big or go home. Except I'm not going home. Not yet, anyway."

"Tease." It was easy to be with her, even when she asked questions about his newfound family.

"It has to be mind-boggling to have a twin. To have that connection with someone. Do you see aspects of yourself when you look at him?"

He had to think about how to answer that. Not because he was choosing his words, but because he hadn't really thought of Reid and himself in that way. What was it like to look at Reid, whom Tate had *shared a womb with*, for God's sake?

"We both gesture with our hands when we talk. Not wildly or anything, but subtly. We do this—" he pressed his index finger and thumb together like he was popping a balloon with a pin "—when we want to make a point. I never paid attention to that until Reid did it. And then I noticed I did it, too. That I've always done it."

"So you make the same gestures even though you haven't been around each other for decades."

"Apparently. It's surreal. I always thought I was an only child and then I meet this stranger and a few dinners later it's like I've known him my whole life."

"I guess in a way, you have." Hayden rested her hand on Tate's thigh.

"He invited me to London for Christmas." Tate took a deep breath. He wasn't sure how he felt about that invitation. "Where my parents live."

"That's exciting," she said, but there was caution in her tone.

"I didn't give him an answer yet, but Reid and Drew—his pregnant fiancée—are going."

"You're going to be an uncle." Her face brightened. "Lucky. I'm an only child. No hope of being an aunt unless I'm made honorary aunt by one of my friends."

And to think he used to be an only child, too. "It's... overwhelming to have this all happening at once."

"I'm sure it is. I bet your adoptive parents are having a hard time letting you navigate the holidays now that they have to share you."

"You have no idea." He rubbed his temple, a headache forming behind his fingers. His mother had cried when he'd told her he wouldn't be home for Thanksgiving or Christmas, and his father had demanded he consider someone other than himself. Tate hadn't argued, simply explaining that he was doing what he had to do. A breath later his father was apologizing and his mother had stopped crying. Tate still felt the sting from their reactions, though. He'd had an almost consuming need to give in to what they wanted. In the end he'd stood his ground.

"I'm sorry. Just tell me to shut up. I didn't mean to encroach on your—"

"I was kidnapped," he interrupted, and Hayden's jaw went slack. She didn't know the whole truth, and he needed her to see the full picture. If only to understand why he was making the decisions he was making "At age three. I was taken from my and my brother's birthday party in London, and our parents never found me again. My adoptive parents assumed the agency they were adopting me from was legitimate until that agency extorted money from them. They suspected something was off, but they wanted a child so badly."

His budding headache took root and throbbed like a truth bomb ready to detonate.

"The Duncans were told my birth parents were dead—they were given falsified death certificates filled out with fake names. Eventually, my real birth parents believed I was dead. They buried an empty casket five years after my disappearance."

"Oh, Tate." Sympathy flooded Hayden's dark eyes.

He continued, monotone. Might as well share it all. "My adoptive parents paid the so-called agency's exorbitant fees without asking too many questions. My mother said she never would've imagined I was kidnapped. She had an inkling that the agency was unscrupulous, but if money was the only thing standing in the way of bringing me home..."

He shook his head. It wasn't their fault. Not really. But he couldn't help blaming them for not acting on their instincts. Had Marion explored that inkling he might've been raised in London rather than California. He might've been returned to his rightful home, to his actual birth parents who were no more than strangers to him now.

And you wouldn't have been raised by the Duncans. Which meant never knowing the family he loved dearly. Never setting foot on Spright Island to build a community that he treasured. Never meeting the people who lived here—Hayden included.

He wasn't sure which thought was more chill-inducing.

Spooked, the deer became suddenly alert, before

turning and darting off into the trees, his white tail a visible exclamation point in the dark. Had his parents been equally afraid of digging for the truth?

"Then a month ago I was in a coffee shop in Seattle, and this guy in front of me in line starts babbling about how I was his twin brother."

Hayden's hand formed a fist and she seemed to keep herself in check. Like she wanted to touch him but didn't know if she should. "You must've been…"

"Terrified," Tate finished for her. "I called my mom after, expecting her to laugh it off. She didn't. And the next night when I had dinner with Claire, I drank a stupid amount of wine and told her everything I just told you, and…"

"She left you."

"Not that night, but eventually. Yes." He gave Hayden a sad smile. "Now's your chance."

But she didn't heed his warning, stand up and put on her coat. She gripped the back of his neck and kissed him soft and long. Achingly gentle. He returned her kiss, tasting on her lips the newfound courage she'd uncovered.

She made him feel strong, confident. All the ways he used to be that had gone missing recently. He felt as if he'd been tossed overboard into a churning sea of uncertainty and was only now clawing his way onto dry land.

"Most complicated one-night stand ever," she said, rubbing her thumb along his bottom lip.

"Is that enough for you?" God knew it was all he had to give. He couldn't rely on the future any longer. Certainty was a myth.

She tilted her head and watched him. "I'm not opposed to two nights."

He smiled. "How about we take it one night at a time?" He was already mentally undressing her, wanting more of the earlier taste she gave him.

She unbuttoned a button on his shirt and then the one under it. "One night at a time."

He covered her lips with a kiss, the sweetness from the marshmallow on her tongue. One night at a time was as unchartered as territory came for him. Completely opposite of how he'd operated before.

He had no idea where they would end up. One night at a time broke every rule he had, every guideline he'd followed previously. Which was exactly what he needed.

Different. New. Exciting.

In a word: *Hayden*.

Eleven

One night turned into two and two into three and three into more. Hayden and Tate had been saying yes to almost three weeks' worth of nights so far.

It was December and Christmas was in full swing at SWC. Colorful lights and garland were wrapped around lampposts, retail shop doors boasted gold-and-green wreaths and holiday music was piped through speakers inside.

Hayden had decorated her small, but pretty, tree in her apartment with red and gold decorations, and the larger one in her studio with silver and blue. She even went through the trouble of hanging outdoor lights for the first time.

As loath as she was to admit it, life really *was* better when she wasn't alone during the holidays.

She'd spent a lot of time at Tate's house, in front

of the fireplace and in his bed. So much time that she hadn't been at her own apartment much, save for running upstairs to change or showering after her classes. With her schedule trimmed back for the holidays, though, she had a decent amount of free time.

She'd finished up her last class of the year ten minutes ago and was just updating her planner and checking her email when the bell over the door dinged to alert her someone was coming in.

Since she knew exactly who that someone was, she didn't bother calling out that she was closed.

Tate looked like the billionaire Arlene had accused him of being, his expensive trousers in deep charcoal gray, his shoes black and shiny. The part of him that deviated was the ever-present dark leather jacket that hung over his muscular, round shoulders.

"Now that's a nice scarf," she commented about the red scarf looped around his neck. She'd purchased it for him, for no reason except she'd seen it and thought of him.

His sexy grin was missing as he stalked toward her in the empty studio, however, causing her nerves to prickle, and not pleasantly.

And since that prickle came with fear that things had changed and she didn't know why or how, she didn't like it at all.

Breathe. He's allowed to have a bad day.

Plus, he was here. That's what mattered.

"What's up?" she asked, forcing a bright tone.

He seemed to snap out of it at the question. "Nothing. The scarf—" he lifted one side of it "—was a gift from an incredibly beautiful woman."

He was joking, that was a good sign. "Should I be jealous?"

He kissed her hello, a long and lingering press of his lips that assuaged her fears some. Maybe she'd over-reacted. It wasn't like she was accustomed to being happy and in a relationship. Getting used to both si-multaneously would take some doing.

Hayden reminded herself not to put too much pres-sure on the outcome. Years ago she'd decided that being on her own was A-okay. She didn't need a family or a marriage, or even a boyfriend, to feel whole. Even so, she couldn't deny that she was happy with Tate. She was going to enjoy it, no matter how finite.

And she was *so* into Tate Duncan. More than any guy she'd ever met. It'd only been three weeks, and already he was more than a friend—way more than a sex buddy. He was just plain *more*, and she'd left it at that in her head. Labeling what they had was danger-ous. Like naming it would lead to its inevitable end sooner rather than later.

"How did the meeting go?" she asked.

Tate had stopped by a planning meeting for the New Year's Eve gala, which consisted of a lush black-tie party with cocktails and dancing.

"Well. Ran into Nick there. He invited us to the Purple Rose for lunch."

Nick was, hands down, Hayden's favorite chef. He made some of freshest, most delicious meals, all using simple ingredients.

"Us?" Without her permission, her heart lifted at the reference that Tate had mentioned her to Nick.

"We're hardly under the radar, Ms. Green." But

Tate's smile told her that he didn't mind they were SWC-official. "Are you available?"

"I am," she said with a smile of her own.

An hour later they were enjoying roasted vegetable–white bean salad, a quinoa bowl and a plate of crispy Brussels sprouts drenched in a sweet Thai dressing.

"As I suspected," Hayden said as she spooned another healthy portion of Brussels sprouts onto her plate. "Nick sold his soul to the devil in exchange for the recipe for this sauce."

Plus it wasn't on the menu yet. She could get used to this sort of special treatment. She hadn't been in the market for a boyfriend, if that's what Tate was, but having one that held the golden key to the city was the way to go.

Tate placed his fork on his table, swiping his mouth with a napkin. His gaze was unfocused, his demeanor shifting abruptly. She was reminded of the mood he'd been in when he stepped into her studio.

"I have something to ask you." His eyebrows compressed.

Even as her heart ka-thumped a worried staccato, Hayden said, "Okay."

"It's a big ask."

"Okay."

"Reid called me this morning, asking again if I'd consider going to London for Christmas." His Adam's apple jumped when he swallowed, and he reached for his water glass. "I've decided to go."

"That's great." She meant it. Meeting his birth parents was a huge leap for him.

"I want you to go with me."

Hayden sagged in her seat, shocked down to her toes. Everything about the way he'd been behaving would have her assuming he'd dump her not...take her to London?

She couldn't say yes to *going to London* with him. Even though she'd wanted to visit England for as long as she could remember.

Meeting his family was *huge*. And at Christmas? That was monumental.

He continued to watch her, waiting for acknowledgment, or maybe for her to shout an exuberant *yes!* Since she didn't know what to say, she sort of repeated his words. "Go with you? To London?"

"Yes. There's more."

More than inviting her to London for Christmas to meet his birth parents? She slicked damp palms on her jeans. She wasn't sure she wanted to know, but for the sake of her sanity, she *had* to know, or else the possibilities would stack themselves to the heavens before falling onto her and crushing her to death.

Calm down. It's not like he's going to propose.

But then he said, "The Singletons are under the assumption that I'm engaged. Because I *was* engaged. Reid knows Claire and I ended, but I asked him not to tell George and Jane that my engagement was off."

Oh, God. *Was* he going to propose?

"Why not tell them?" she croaked, her mind and heart racing like they were vying for first place.

"I'm not sure." His frown deepened. "I was concerned they'd think I wasn't doing well, I guess? That they would assume their son's life was unraveling because of the news. I guess I didn't want them to worry."

He was one of the kindest men she'd ever met. Even amidst the turmoil in his own life, he was looking out for those who loved him. Even those he had no memory of knowing.

"If you don't have a passport, I can pay to have it expedited for you."

"I have a passport," she said. "What is it, exactly, that you need from me?"

He nodded, his expression an unsure mix of dread and concern. "If they assume you're my fiancée—if they even remember I have one—all you have to do is not argue. You don't have to pretend your name is Claire, or anything."

"Good. I wouldn't." She quirked her lips and Tate's mouth shifted into a smile.

"I don't want to keep you from your plans, but it'd be a huge favor for me. Your travel and incidentals would be covered."

She started to say he didn't have to do that but with her light work schedule and shopping for the holidays she hadn't exactly stashed away a few thou for a trip to another country.

"I've always wanted to go to London."

She might be sweating the fact that Tate, who was basically a really meaningful fling, was sort of proposing to her and asking her to go to a foreign country, but she couldn't not be there for him when he needed her. Going to celebrate Christmas with a bunch of strangers might be weird for her, but she imagined for him, it'd be downright uncomfortable.

Plus, visiting London would be a dream come true. The alternative would be going home to Seattle to endure her grandmother's drunkenness, her mother's scrambling after her like a servant and her father's apathy.

Tate was still watching her carefully, as if he was deciding whether or not to sweeten the pot by offering something more. He didn't have to. She wanted to be with him, and this was a unique situation.

"I'll do it."

"Yeah?" He grinned, the agony from earlier sweeping away with that smile.

Tate deserved a win, and, dammit so did she. If pretending to be his fiancée would give them both a sense of triumph, why the hell not?

But a small voice in her head whispered, *so many reasons*.

Twelve

Reid and Drew had flown to London two days ago. There was a reason Tate didn't sync his flight with his twin's: he wanted to keep his stay in the UK as brief as possible. With the excuse of work—partially true—he'd instead booked his and Hayden's international flight to arrive at 11:15 a.m. December 23. That gave them the day to hide away to rest, and then they could emerge for cocktail hour and dinner before ducking away again to sleep. Then all he'd have to endure was Christmas Eve and Christmas Day before flying home the next morning. Which, thanks to an eight-hour time difference, would land them in Seattle just two hours after they left England.

He'd booked first-class business tickets on the flight out, not because he was planning on working but because they were the best seats the airline had to offer.

Hayden was doing him a solid by joining him—he wanted to make sure she felt special.

When Hayden sat in her seat next to a bulky armrest-slash-desk, her eyebrows were so high on her forehead it was almost comical. "Tate."

She took in the cabin around her, which consisted of thirty business-class "pods," each with its own private, wraparound seat dividers. There was a divider that could separate his and Hayden's seats as well, but he'd lowered it the second they found their seats.

"Sorry, this was the nicest seat the airline had."

"Smart-ass." Subtly, she shook her head, her smile tolerant. "I usually sit in the middle of coach with my knees smashed into the seat in front of me."

She stretched her legs out, unable to touch the pod in front of her with her toes. Then her smile faded. "It's too much."

"Let's revisit that claim five hours into a nine-and-a-half-hour flight." He lifted an eyebrow. "You'll be thanking me for copious legroom and a chair that reclines."

"And my own TV." She gestured at the screen in front of her. "And tray table, and—" She lifted a black bag labeled Amenity Kit and held it up to show him.

"Sleep mask, lavender spray and a Casper-brand pillow and fleece blanket."

She laughed, an effervescent sound, and the tightness in his chest eased. There would be a lot of people and overwhelming circumstances to deal with shortly after they landed at Heathrow, but for right now, he had it easy. With Hayden.

She'd made this trip better already and it hadn't

started yet. Plus, watching her wide eyes gobble up the luxury that had become pedestrian to him was a good reminder of how far he'd come. The dose of confidence and self-assuredness would go a long way when he was a stranger in a strange land... Except it wasn't a strange land. It was his *hometown*.

Would that ever sink in?

Hayden was oohing and ahhing over the lavender spray and mentioned again how fluffy the pillow was, and he had to grin.

"You're easy to spoil, Ms. Green."

Her cheeks pinked. "I'm acting like a total country mouse, aren't I?"

"A little, but I'm enjoying it." He'd never done without. Trips he'd taken with his family had always been in first class or via private flight. Seeing this experience through fresh eyes was damned refreshing. Just like the rest of her.

"I can't help it. It's new to me." She narrowed her eyes in faux suspicion. "Are you making sure I'm not going to back out at the last second? Have you heard all sorts of horrifying secrets about your family? Am I in for the ride of my life?"

"The opposite. Reid gushes over them. And Drew hasn't met them but she says she's spent a lot of time on the phone with Reid's, um, our mother, Jane." He paused while that soaked in. "Anyway, Drew loves her already, and she hasn't met her."

"That's good news." Hayden's encouragement was careful, but Tate had a feeling they'd survive this awkward holiday regardless of what he had to face. At least he wouldn't be facing it alone.

He appreciated the hell out of her for being here.

It wasn't something he'd successfully put into words, but he hoped the first-class flight, the trip to London and every last way he planned on worshipping her in the bedroom would say what he couldn't: That there was no one he'd rather navigate this patch of his life with other than Hayden.

One day at a time.

Seven hours into the flight Hayden was feeling the fatigue of traveling tenfold. The longest flight she'd been on had been a five-hour flight to Toronto for a yoga conference last year. She could thank that trip for her having a passport.

She'd already been to the bathroom and had moved around to stretch her legs. Even the roomy pod, complete with seat and desk, couldn't cure her craving for movement. She struck a few poses as best she could from her chair, regardless of who watched. Though, she doubted anyone was paying attention to her or her seated warrior pose. There were only thirty seats in this section of the plane, and she assumed everyone desired privacy first and foremost. It was by far the best way to travel.

She would've liked to give Tate at least *some* money for her travel expenses, no matter how trivial. Yes, they were dating, but this went beyond their agreement to take things as they came. But each time she brought it up, he shook his head denoting the end of the discussion. An hour into their flight she'd tried again and his, "It's a gift, Hayden, stop asking," told her she had surpassed insistence and tiptoed into ungratefulness.

She couldn't help it. Financial arguments had been commonplace in her family's home especially since her grandmother drank away every dollar she wrapped her fist around, leaving her wellbeing to Hayden's parents.

Hayden hadn't grown up with a healthy view of much of anything as a kid. As an adult she'd studied her backside off trying to learn how to save and invest for her future. Since the bulk of care and concern from her mother was lavished on her father and grandmother, Hayden had been on her own.

She'd learned to care for herself, knowing no one else would take care of her. It was the harder path, but at least reliable. It was also the main reason she'd chose to stay unmarried. Trusting herself was easy. Trusting others, not so much.

Tate, reclined in his seat, arms folded over his chest, was asleep. She watched his chest lift and fall and considered how much she'd trusted him already, without realizing she was doing it.

Anyone would assume he was peacefully snoozing except for the furrow in his brow. He was worried about meeting them—his parents. She couldn't imagine how she'd feel if she'd found out she had a whole other family who lived in London.

Relieved, probably, she thought with a bittersweet smile.

Thirteen

When Hayden first laid eyes on Tate's brother, Reid, she thought, *My God, there really are two of them.*

They weren't identical twins, but there was no denying the set of their mouths and—Tate was right—they both made the same gestures when they talked.

In the back seat of Reid's rental car, she sat next to his fiancée Drew while the guys carried on a conversation up front.

"They're both so attractive it's stupefying," Drew stated. "Don't you think?"

The question was asked at a near whisper, even though the guys were chattering loud enough that they likely hadn't overheard.

"It doesn't take much to stupefy me after that flight," Hayden joked. The truth, had she been forced to admit it, was that 100 percent of the attraction coming from her was aimed directly at Tate.

"No kidding." Drew snorted, and like the rest of her, it was darling. "We arrived three days ago, and my body is just now accepting that I'm supposed to be awake."

"So by the time I'm used to the time change, I'll be on my way back home."

"You're seriously leaving on Boxing Day? Criminal!" Drew clutched her nonexistent pearls. "It is sad that you're not staying longer, though."

Hayden felt similarly. She liked Drew, even having only known her for a few minutes. The other woman was both scrappy and easygoing. Hayden didn't know much about how Drew and Reid got together, except that she was the little sister of one of Reid's best friends. Hayden would bet there was a story there. She'd have to extract details from Drew over dinner.

"Hey! I heard you're engaged!" Drew exclaimed.

"Uh…"

"*Pretending* to be engaged, love," Reid corrected his fiancée, throwing a wink at her in the rearview mirror. "I told you that."

"I *know*. Mind your own business up there, Gorgeous Inc. That's his new nickname." Drew pursed her lips. "I guess though, if Reid is the CEO of Gorgeous Inc., Tate has to be, at the very least, COO." She glanced first at Reid's profile, then Tate's. "Stupefying."

Hayden giggled, but it led to a yawn. She was feeling every hour of their lengthy travel.

"Do you want coffee?" Drew offered, clearly discerning what that yawn was about. "It's easier to find tea here, but there are a few really good shops that serve both. We stopped by one when we finished Christmas shopping yesterday."

"Mum is serving tea when we arrive." Reid said as he drove past pubs and shops downtown. "Can't rob her of that."

Tate rubbed his palms down his dark jeans, and Hayden thought she saw his shoulders stiffen. No doubt the mention of his "mum" had set him on edge.

Reid, consummate entertainer, launched into his tour guide voice and pointed out a few buildings beyond the car's window.

Drew leaned closer to Hayden, keeping her voice low. "I can't imagine how difficult this must be for Tate."

"Yes."

"And you." Sincerity swam in the other brunette's dark gaze. "If you need anyone to talk to while you're here…about family stuff or girl stuff…or *engagement* stuff."

Hayden laughed. "You're not going to give up on that, are you?"

"Nope." Drew grinned, seemingly pleased with herself, and pleased in general. She palmed her still-flat, pregnant belly. "I'm just saying, you can't predict where you'll end up with these Singleton boys. Right, Gorgeous, Inc.?"

The look Reid sent through the rearview was a smolder if Hayden had ever seen one. And when Tate peeked over his shoulder at her, that look held a certain smolder for her as well.

Those Singleton boys, indeed.

* * *

Tate took in the rows of houses they drove past, most tightly packed in next to each other. Having not been here past the age of three, he had no recollection of the area. Nothing looked familiar and the foreignness only made him long for his parents' home in California. His chest grew tight. He'd never been a homesick kid, but he felt that way now.

The cocktail of excitement and nerves over meeting the man and woman who'd created him had been shaken, stirred and then thrown into a blender for good measure. He'd had a million silent discussions with himself on the flight over about expectations, reasoning that this meeting didn't have to be anything more than cordial. But it was hard not to have expectations when Reid went on and on about their parents. He meant well, but it'd almost been too much to absorb for Tate.

"They're getting on well," Reid said. "We'll have to keep an eye on that, brother, in case they decide to team up on us."

Reid pulled into a long asphalt driveway flanked by short, decorative stone pillars. "Here we are."

The Singleton house was in Berkshire, about half an hour from the airport, and sat on three acres of land which backed up to the very wooded area Tate had been dragged to when he was a toddler.

He repressed a shudder.

"Mum's bloody gorgeous, by the way." Reid smirked, proud. "She was a fashion model in her twenties, not that she looks a day past thirty-seven." He threw the car into Park and faced Tate. "Mate. Welcome home." Then Reid lightened the heavy sentiment with, "I've already warned Mum not to smother you. You're welcome."

Tate had to hand it to his brother—Reid hadn't acted as if this was strange for a while now. Ironically, that made this entirely strange situation easier to accept.

As the four of them climbed from the car and approached the house, the dark wood front door with iron handles swung open.

He'd seen photos of Jane and George, but nothing could have prepared him for seeing his birth parents in the flesh for the first time in decades.

"Silver fox, am I right?" Drew murmured under her breath to Hayden. "His mom's hot, too."

Hayden replied, but Tate couldn't hear anything save the blood rushing past his eardrums. His poised mother was stationed at the threshold, dressed in white slacks and a cowl-necked gray sweater. She held on to Tate's father, who wore a casual suit and looked much younger than his stately name implied. Jane's hair was stylishly gray, but George's maintained most of its dark brown with only a feathering of gray at the temples.

Tate took in every detail of the pair as he walked on stiff legs. Reid mentioned the traffic going easy before gently gripping his—*their*—mother's shoulders and guiding her inside. Before Tate stepped over the threshold, he felt Hayden's hand in his.

"Piece of cake," she whispered, looking beautiful but jet-lagged. Tate might be in unfamiliar territory but she'd become familiar. He would be here, facing this moment alone, if it wasn't for her.

He squeezed her fingers with his, unable to tell her

what it meant to him that she was here, but hoping she knew anyway. Her tired wink suggested she might.

He'd make sure she had time to rest during the next few days. He pulled her to walk beside him and stole a kiss before following everyone inside. Reid led his mother into the entryway and then stood next to Drew.

George offered Tate a palm, the first to break the invisible wall between them. Looking into his father's face was like seeing someone you thought you might know but couldn't remember from where. Tate gripped George's hand.

"Good handshake, son. I'm your father, George Singleton. This is your mother, Jane." He cupped his wife's shoulder as she began to cry. Pretty at first, her high cheekbones and full lips barely shifting from their neutral positions, but a moment later, tears fell and that perfect bone structure seemed to dissolve.

Her outstretched arms shook when she reached for Tate. "Please, may I?" Her voice was broken, and Tate wasn't far behind, nodding his acceptance as tears blurred his vision.

He held his mother, expecting awkwardness, but it never came. Odd as it was to feel a connection with her, he did. The same way he'd felt it with Reid since the first moment he saw him in that coffee shop. As if a connection deep in his soul had been forged eons ago.

"Oh, my Wesley," she murmured repeatedly as she held on to him. "My sweet Wesley." She must have felt his arms go rigid, because she abruptly pulled away and corrected herself. "Tate. Tate is your name."

"They're both my names." He'd come to accept that

recently. Easier now that the woman who'd carried him in her womb was standing in the circle of his arms.

Jane embraced him again, holding on for a long moment. A few other sniffs sounded in the room—from the direction of Drew and Hayden if Tate wasn't mistaken.

Jane let go of Tate, nodding with finality, her tears no longer falling. "One thing's for certain," she said as she studied his face. "You're much better looking than your brother."

"Hey!" Reid protested. The rest of them laughed and the tension that had built receded some.

It was *really* good to laugh.

"All right, then. Tea." Jane clapped her hands and led them farther into the house. Rich, caramel brown floors matched the doorframes and windowsills, and the walls were painted a soft white. The color palette was mostly burgundies and pine greens, and everywhere Tate looked was a reminder of nature. *Like my house*, he thought as he admired a piece of petrified wood in a slightly misshapen hand-thrown clay bowl.

"I made it. It's rubbish," Jane said of the bowl, bypassing it to walk to a cart in the corner of the room.

"So's what's in it," George agreed, his tone teasing. "A stick that's turned into a rock."

"Tate has petrified wood in his house," Hayden said, meeting his eyes and then Jane's. "You two have that in common." She stroked his arm with a hand as they lowered onto a jewel-toned settee, but then rose a moment later to help his mother serve.

"…lucky to have such a caring fiancée," Tate heard his mother say.

Hayden shot a quick glance to Tate, her expression no doubt matching his own. She recovered smoothly, flashing his mother a grin and offering a generic, polite response. "Thank you, Jane. I'm happy to help."

"I hear you own a nature preserve," George said, drawing Tate's attention from his fake fiancée.

Hayden handed Tate a cup of tea and sat with him and he renewed the promise he'd made to himself on the trip over. He was definitely making time to show Hayden his appreciation later.

Fourteen

"Your parents are sort of incredible." Hayden unpacked her suitcase, stashing her clothes in the dresser in the guest bedroom.

On that count, Tate had to agree. The weirdest part about meeting them was that they no longer felt like strangers. They'd discussed Spright Island, Jane and George both eager to hear of Tate's success with the community. Jane abashedly admitted that she'd "Googled it" and was "quite impressed."

He'd always been proud of the work he'd done there. The wellness community was his passion, but also his legacy. He'd never thought much about having a family of his own, always focusing instead on work. Claire had been equally focused on her career and stated she'd never wanted to have children. After having met the members of his actual family tree, though, Tate had briefly entertained the idea of having a family of his own. He supposed that was inevitable considering the circumstances.

Hayden hid her suitcase in the closet, yawning as she shut the bedroom door. He wondered if she wanted children. She'd never mentioned it before, but given the hints that her family was rife with conflict, maybe she didn't. It wasn't the kind of discussion two people having a day-to-day affair would have, but he couldn't stop the vision of a little boy with dark hair and his blue eyes. Or twins.

"Jesus." He pulled a hand down his face to staunch the thoughts.

"I know. I'm tired, too." Hayden yawned again and he was glad she'd assumed he was tired rather than considering her potentially bearing his children. Maybe he could blame fatigue on his thoughts. They certainly weren't par for course.

Is any of this?

"Why don't you stay up here and rest." The guest room was hidden away at the back of the upstairs hall-way, and he knew his parents wouldn't mind Hayden not showing for cocktail hour. Besides, it'd been George that had had invited Tate and Reid for brandy. Pregnant Drew had begged off to bed and his mother told Tate she'd happily join Hayden for a nip, but only if Hayden wasn't too tired. "Jane meant what she said when she told you to do what you like."

Hayden tilted her head and studied him, a spark of interest in her eyes despite the fatigue. "Do you think you'll ever be comfortable calling her Mom? Or Mum, as Reid calls her?"

Tate sucked in a breath. He guessed it wasn't that alarming to be thinking of having a family. He was surrounded by family and piecing the relationships together as best he could.

"Maybe someday," he said, but oddly that felt like a betrayal to his adoptive mother.

"You're handling this really well." Hayden palmed his cheek.

Placing his hands on her hips, Tate pulled her closer, and she draped her forearms over his shoulders. She fit there, in his embrace. Claire hadn't fit in his arms like she was meant to be there—a detail he'd always overlooked. And now that he'd met George and Jane and Reid Singleton, he wondered if in hindsight he'd find that he never fit with his family in California, either.

"Deep thoughts?"

"How do you know where you belong? Is it with the people who are familiar, or the people who are related?"

"That's a whopper, Tate Duncan," She paused to consider. "I used to feel comfortable in chaos, but now I crave a stable environment. In your very unique case, I don't think you'll have to choose. You have room in your life for your adoptive parents and your birth parents, for Reid and Drew, and for your new niece or nephew when he or she is born."

And you.

Pretending to be engaged to Hayden, pretending they had a future with "forever" implied, it wasn't hard to picture her there during his brother's wedding, the birth of a niece or nephew, or even a vacation to California to meet his adoptive parents.

That, too, felt dangerous, but this was also a safe place to consider the possibility of what life would be like if he and Hayden were truly engaged.

How it'd be expected to linger in their shared bedroom...

"How tired are you?" Tate lowered his mouth to her neck.

"Mmm," she purred.

He took to her lips for a brief kiss that didn't stay that way. Sliding his tongue along hers was the foolproof cure for jet lag. He backed her toward the bed.

"Tate," she whispered, and he was sure "we can't" would follow.

"Don't tell me to stop." He needed her. Needed to ground himself in the only reality that made sense right now. If there was one component that wasn't pretend, it was their explosive chemistry.

She raised and lowered one eyebrow, suddenly alert. "I was going to say brandy with George and Reid can wait."

"Hell, yes, it can."

She'd dressed for dinner in a long-sleeved black shirt made from material that held the slightest shimmer. He slipped a hand beneath it and along her smooth skin.

She tipped her head back, her dark hair falling over her shoulders while his hands explored her full breasts over the smooth cups of her bra.

Her moan of approval spurred him on. And like that first time he was with her, he didn't want to rush. Brandy with his family be damned.

He made short work of stripping her of her shirt and bra. Cupping her breasts, he thumbed her nipples and then kissed the tips of each. Her hands explored his hair, wrecking it. He took that as encouragement and continued circling one nipple with his tongue.

He unbuttoned her dark pants, slipping his hand past the waistband of her panties to tease her smooth folds. Spreading that wetness over her clit, he guided his fingers back and forth, until Hayden's hands clutched his shoulders and her moans elevated to bleats of pleasure.

Yanking his head from her chest, she kissed him with ferocity, none of her earlier fatigue present. He tenderly stroked her into her first orgasm. Watching her mouth round in pleasure and her beautiful face contort wouldn't be a sight he'd soon forget.

She shuddered in his arms, and he supported her weight, bracing her waist and kissing a trail from her jaw to her ear.

"You're so fucking gorgeous when you do that," he rasped. "This time, do it again, but with me inside you."

"Sounds good to me." She smiled. A challenge.

He lifted her into his arms and tossed her onto the bed. She bounced, stifling her laugh with a hand over her lips while he tugged off her heeled shoes and pants.

She daintily scooted back, folding her long legs to one side and looking up at him sexily. She was like every wet dream he'd ever had, only better—because she was here. She was real. And he was *really* going to enjoy coaxing forth her next orgasm.

Tate took off his shirt, and Hayden's dark eyes flared. That she looked at him the way he looked at her—like she couldn't believe how damn lucky she was to have him naked—hardened his erection and sharpened his desire.

He finished undressing and climbed over her, tickling her lips with a series of gentle kisses before trailing his mouth down her neck to her breasts. He made a pit stop at each one—he'd never be able to resist the lure of her perfect nipples—and then made himself comfortable between her thighs.

Ruined.

Tate had ruined her for anyone else. Which was alarming, since she didn't spend much time considering a man permanently being around for sex, or dating, or…anything, really.

But, she wasn't above having fun.

Which was what this is, she reminded herself sternly.

George and Jane, and even Reid and Drew who knew the engagement was for show, had treated Hayden like family tonight. There was a part of her that had basked in that attention. At the idea of being a part of a family that genuinely seemed to want for each other, not from each other.

But Tate wasn't a permanent fixture. This was a fairy tale. One where she'd been whisked to London by a wealthy prince—one who *really* knew how to use his freaking tongue.

The sound of the condom wrapper being torn open jolted her out of her post-orgasmic bliss.

"Wait!"

Tate looked almost alarmed at her outburst, which was sort of funny.

"Let's hold off on this part." She took the condom from his hand. "There's something I wanted to do first."

Shoving him onto his back, she pressed a kiss to

first one pectoral and then the other and positioned herself over him. As she kissed her way down his torso, Tate grew reverently silent. She knew he'd figured out her intentions the moment he scooped her hair into his hands and watched her work.

And oh, did she *work*.

She held his shaft at the base, flicking him a sultry glance while licking the tip of his cock. His mouth dropped open, the tendons in his neck standing out in stark relief.

He smelled of soap from their earlier—and sadly, separate—showers, and the musky smell that was his and his alone.

She alternated with teasing licks and loving kisses and then swallowed him whole, tickling his balls while the air sawed out of his lungs in uneven gasps.

Moments before she would have swallowed his release, he tugged her hair, still wrapped in his fists. "Hayden."

When she didn't stop right away, his voice grew gruff, more demanding, *"Hayden."*

She let him go with a soft pop, licking her lips. "Fine. I'll stop, but only bec—"

Without warning, he flipped her to her back and was over her in an instant. She yelped in surprise then slapped a hand over her mouth. The house was large, but not *that* large. No need to broadcast that she was upstairs shagging the Singletons' newfound son.

"Condom," she reminded him as he nudged her entrance with his very hard member.

"Right. Of course." He blinked once, then twice like he was trying to bring his brain back online. He rolled on the condom in record time and, before her next breath, entered her in one long, slow slide. Buried to the root, he paused to blow out a careful, measured breath.

"You okay, COO of Gorgeous Inc.?" She feathered his hair from his forehead, and he offered a narrow-eyed glare. "COO? Founder? Which do you prefer?"

"I prefer—" he slid out and then in again "—for you to call me by my name. Repeatedly. And with growing enthusiasm," he added as he continued moving.

"Tate." He seemed to gain strength as she repeated his name over and over. As if he'd needed, more than anything, that reminder of who he was. As if hearing his name had anchored him.

"Come for me, Hayden." He lifted her calf, and she stretched her leg to rest it easily on his shoulder. The angle made it easier for him to hit her G-spot, which he had a knack for finding.

"There," she said with a gasp. Damn, he was good.

"One more for me. Then I'll let you sleep for a few hours."

He grinned, and she returned it. Her smile fell when she felt the telltale building of a showstopper of an orgasm.

"Tate." She continued worshipping as she gripped the blankets with kneading fists. Her nipples pebbled in the cool bedroom air even as sweat beaded his forehead from his workout.

The fourth stroke was the charm.

She dissolved, the release hitting her so hard she squeezed her eyes shut to absorb the impact. He wasn't far behind her, growling his release. He came to a jerky stop moments before collapsing on top of her.

His weight pressed her into the mattress, a thin sheen of sweat sticking his chest to hers. "By far my favorite work out is having sex with you."

"Agreed." She swept a hand through his hair and kissed his temple.

He left to deal with the condom, but by the time he returned, her eyes refused to stay open. She was vaguely aware of the sound of him pulling on his clothes, barely awake when he feathered a kiss on her cheek.

The last words she remembered was his whispered promise of, "Rest up. You'll need your strength for later."

Fifteen

"He had no idea who you were?" Hayden leaned closer to Drew at the tightly packed bar.

When they'd first stepped into the Churchill, she'd been agape with wonder. The outside of the building was draped with Christmas trees. "Eighty of them and eighteen thousand fairy lights," Reid had shared. From that point on, the place had fascinated her.

Hanging from the ceiling were numerous beaten-copper pots, pans and lights, and at one point she spotted a guitar case and even an accordion. As its name suggested, the Churchill was dripping with memorabilia, in memory of the man after which it was named. The walls were wooden and dotted with framed photos and paintings, the tables and chairs well worn from plenty of use.

"There's no better place to be than Church on

Christmas Eve," Reid had told Tate, looping a broth-
erly arm around his neck as he'd dragged him inside.

Hayden was ridiculously happy for Tate. He had a
fun, boisterous, lovable family. She could see clearly
that his mother had wanted to accompany him out tonight only to be close to him awhile longer. And who
could blame her? The woman had gone decades believing her other son was *deceased*. In the end George
had wrangled Jane in, encouraging her to "let the lads
and lasses have their fun."

Drew circled the straws in her club soda with lime
before confirming Hayden's question. "Reid had no
clue it was me."

"Then what?" Hayden was on the edge of her seat
hearing how Drew and Reid had bumped into each
other at a work conference. She stirred her own club
soda with lime, content with the mocktail and Drew's
company. She listened intently as Drew told her about
the huge crush she'd had on Reid when she was sixteen
years old and how running into him again was her very
narrow window to properly seduce him.

"So I'm lying in his hotel room bed fast asleep and
he does this—" Drew snapped her fingers in Hayden's
face "—and literally *scolds* me for not telling him who
I was!"

Hayden laughed. It'd be a story for the grandkids,
without a doubt… An edited version, but still.

Drew was beaming, glowing. Even though half her
story was shouted so as to be heard over a rowdy group
of *lads* chugging down their ciders and ales.

The patrons of Churchill had worn their Christmas
finery. For most of the ladies, sparkly dresses—one

lass wore an elf costume—and the guys, including Reid and Tate, wore funny hats. Reid, a court jester hat and he'd talked Tate into the one shaped like a giant pint of ale.

"He's doing well, Tate," Drew pulled her eyes away from their guys to say. "I've been trying not to watch him with George and Jane, but it's so beautiful to see them together. And when Reid joins the mix…" Her eyelashes fluttered. "Sorry. Hormones."

"You don't have to explain. I've felt that same sort of emotion being around them. Tate's doing amazingly well."

"I remember the first time I had that look in my eye. It's unique to a woman falling in love."

Hayden tried not to overreact, but she was relatively certain her shocked expression rivaled the one she'd worn when she stepped into Church for the first time tonight. Except instead of awe over garland and pinecones, flickering candles in lanterns and sleigh bells strewn hither and yon, her shock was due to her inability to agree with her new friend.

"It's not love."

"Oh." Drew was uncharacteristically chagrined. "Sorry. I didn't mean to assume…"

Hayden waved a hand to cut off Drew's needless apology. "I can see how you'd draw that conclusion. We have a great time together. He asked me to come here and support him, and I couldn't turn down a friend."

Though *friend* seemed a lame word for what they had been doing together in bed every time they were alone. It sounded lame saying it out loud, too, but if Drew noticed, she was too polite to point it out.

"I'm glad he has you. No matter how you define it. And there's no need to define anything, is there? It's Christmas!" Drew lifted her glass, and Hayden tapped her own against it.

On the other side of the bar, the guys sat close to the fireplace, glasses of bourbon or some kind of brown liquid in hand. Reid tossed his head back and laughed, his throat bobbing, and Tate swiped his eyes as he laughed along with him. Hayden was hit with the oddest sense of pleasure at seeing Tate happy. And not the way she might mildly appreciate someone enjoying themselves. More like she was *invested* in him. Her assuredness about not being in love with him didn't stop her from having feelings that were, while not love, definitely love-*like*.

If there was a real fiancé in Hayden's life, Tate would be the ideal candidate.

Tate sat by the fireplace while Reid fetched refills at the bar. On the way he stopped and placed a hand on Hayden's shoulder and smiled down at her. When she replied with an eye roll, Reid winked.

They'd accepted her, his family. His parents, his brother and Drew. The same way they'd accepted him into their lives. There were rough patches, of course. Awkward moments where the air was stale and no one spoke. But ultimately someone thought of something to say, and it was always in order to help Tate feel at home.

His mother had been asking about wedding plans almost nonstop. "Let me know the date as soon as you're certain," she'd said. "I'll book a flight."

I'll book a flight had been Jane Singleton's mantra since Tate arrived. She was anxious to come to the States, and when Tate agreed at lunch that he'd enjoy showing her around Spright Island, she'd promptly pressed her lips together to quell more tears.

Her crying over him made him uncomfortable, but he understood. He felt as if he'd been robbed, and yet at the same time he wouldn't trade his childhood or his adoptive parents for anything in the world.

Hayden turned her head to look over at him and he waved. She smiled, demurely at first, but then her teeth stabbed her lower lip to keep away a full grin.

My fiancée, he thought when he returned her smile. What had he been thinking asking her to play the role? She was great at it, though. So great that it wasn't hard to imagine her in that role for real. But the timing was so off it wasn't even funny. He was scrambling to keep his life sewn together at the seams and Hayden... He kept referring back to their conversation the first night they were together. One night at a time had been the promise—a reprieve for them both.

Pretending was fine. Short-term. *Fun*. But reality came with an entirely new set of rules.

"Cheers." Reid returned and handed Tate one of the drinks. "Hayden is gorgeous and funny and you're not likely to do better." Reid's cheeks puffed as he held the liquor in them for a beat before swallowing and wincing. "Holy hellfire." He coughed.

Tate opted for a sip rather than a gulp.

"I never saw myself married or a dad, but it's about to happen for me. I'm one of those happy idiots I used to feel sorry for." Reid was more careful taking his next drink. "And before you accuse me of trying to induct you into the married people hall of fame, just know that I have no agenda other than your happiness."

Rare was the moment Reid was sincere, but he appeared so as he held his glass aloft. Even wearing the jester hat.

"I appreciate you looking out for me." Tate sat back into the stuffed chair. "What Hayden and I have now, it's working. It's easy. Simple."

Tate nodded, liking the sound of both of those words. Easy and simple wasn't something his life had been lately.

"Simple has its merits," Reid said, but it sounded like a line. Something to say to fill the air rather than the truth, which reflected in blue eyes that matched Tate's own.

Outside the Singleton home, Tate stood in the backyard, a brisk wind stinging his reddened cheeks. He'd gone to bed around 1:00 a.m., after several glasses of the burning liquid Reid kept bringing him. He'd come back here, passed out and then woke at 3:30 a.m., his heart racing like it was trying to escape his chest.

After three big glasses of water—one of them with an aspirin chaser—Tate wandered outside. The inground pool was draped with a black tarp, closed this time of year. He had vague thoughts of swimming in it, of losing a toy and of his mother diving in after it wearing all her clothes.

He didn't know how much of the memory was memory or how much was his mind desperately trying to connect the dots of his checkered past. Bits of information were missing and colored in with other bits from an entirely different life. He'd yet to piece himself together.

"Wesl—Tate," came his mother's voice from behind him. "Darling, what are you doing?" She bundled a thick parka around her. "It's freezing out here, you'll catch your—"

"Death?" he finished for her. "Too late."

She gave him a light shove in the arm. "Comedian like your brother. Bloody hell! It really is freezing out here."

"We can go in."

"No, no it's fine." She assessed him, something sad in her eyes before she said, "Your adoptive parents contacted us."

He felt the blood rush from his cheeks. He'd had no idea.

"Don't be angry. We contacted them first, hoping if we reached out, they'd reply. I begged Marion—ah, your mother—not to say anything to you. By the look on your face, I assume she complied."

"She didn't tell me." He felt his worlds colliding, fearing that collision and at the same time anxiously anticipating it. He couldn't be two people the rest of his life. At some point he'd have to accept that he was Tate *and* Wesley. Son of Marion and William *and* son of George and Jane.

"I wanted to…understand, I suppose," Jane said. "They're lovely. And as much as I wanted to rage at the couple who kept my son from me all those years, I realize it's not their fault they loved you so fiercely. At least that's what my therapist says I'm supposed to feel." Her mouth quirked. "But I love you, Wes—

Tate. And that means I will prioritize your happiness above my own."

A surge of emotion pushed against his rib cage. After a month of damming it up, only allowing it to release at a trickle, he was due for a tsunami.

His chin shook as another memory crawled out of the recesses of his mind. Jane jumping into the pool after his favorite stuffed toy. He hadn't imagined it. It wasn't made up. The memory was from his toddler-height point of view. And when Jane handed it back sopping wet, he'd cried more and George had helped Jane to her feet, his rumbling laughter encompassing them.

It was *real*, his life here in London. No longer a fuzzy impression he was trying to bring into focus.

"Call me Wesley, Mum," he wrapped an arm around his mother. "That's the name you gave me."

This time when she cried, he held on and cried with her. For the many years they'd lost, and the many years, God willing, they had left.

Sixteen

Dinner was set on the Singleton table, the candles lit, tablecloth spread, and the poinsettia table markers next to embroidered cloth napkins. The Christmas tree was bedazzled with lights in the corner, though Jane mentioned to Hayden they didn't often buy a tree.

"It's a special occasion," Jane had said with a warm smile.

George and Jane sat at either end of the mahogany table while Drew and Reid took their seats side by side. Hayden settled in next to Tate, surprised that spending the holiday away from home, and in a strikingly different environment, hadn't made her feel out of place. She suspected the Singletons had something to do with that—all of them.

Her family holidays were hectic and loud, and not in the charming way. Usually her mother was arguing with her grandmother, who was pouring her third cock-tail before dinner. Mom's cooking was good, though—Hayden wouldn't begrudge her that. But one look at the Singleton spread hinted that Jane knew her way around the kitchen, as well.

A whole turkey was the centerpiece, carved in neat slices and glistening with butter, its skin a crisp golden brown. Sides of diced potatoes and onions, stuffing—though it looked more like hush puppies to Hayden—and vegetables like cabbage, parsnips and a dish of green peas filled in the gaps.

"Right, then. Let's get started." George unfurled his napkin and held out his hands on either side of him. After a beat, Drew and Hayden gathered that they should each take hold of the patriarch's hands for prayer. Hayden held Tate's hand and he in turn held his mother's, who gripped Reid's fingers as he reached for Drew's.

The prayer was brief and proper, and by the time the word *Amen* was uttered, there wasn't a dry eye in the house. Could've had something to do with George giving thanks for "Wesley" being home. "For the first time in nearly three decades," Tate's father had said, "both my sons are under this roof again."

"Gravy," Jane announced, dousing her plate of food with the stuff before passing it on. Hayden politely took the dish from Tate after he'd put some on his potatoes before handing it to George without partaking.

"No sense in watching your waistline, love," George teased with a wink. "All of the veg on this table have been cooked in duck fat." He offered the dish back as though passing on the gravy wasn't an option. She put a dollop on her potatoes. When in Rome, and all that.

Dinner was delicious, if heavy, and once the meal was finished, no one moved to scurry from the table. Typically, at her house, her mother had the food in the fridge the very moment the last plate was cleared. Here, though, Jane made no move to rush around putting food away. Instead she tossed her napkin onto the table saying, "Crackers! I nearly forgot the crackers!"

"Crackers?" Tate asked, and Hayden shared his mild alarm. After stuffing themselves with a rich, two-helpings-of-everything Christmas dinner, who could possibly have room for crackers.

"Oh! I've been wanting to do this!" Drew applauded from her seat.

Jane came out from under the tree with gift-wrapped oblong paper packages tied with ribbons on both ends. They looked like giant, festively wrapped Tootsie Rolls.

"Tradition," Reid explained to the three Americans. He took the gift his mother passed out and explained. "I hold one end, Drew holds the other." A delighted Drew gripped one end of the wrapping. "And then we pull."

A small cracking sound came and the paper tore. Out fell a bauble and a few bits of folded paper. "Looks like I've won a ring." Reid, pleased with his trinket, stuffed it onto his pinky, the purple stone set in plastic not exactly his style. He then unfolded a gold crepe-like paper crown, which he proudly perched on his head. "There, now. I'm ready for my joke."

He reached for the square of paper on the table and read, "What do Santa's little helpers learn at school?" When no one answered, he shared, "The elf-abet."

Jane, George and Reid chuckled. Drew raised an eyebrow. "These are supposed to be bad jokes, right?"

"Oh, the worst." Reid kissed her. "Now yours. Come on then." Drew's cracker held a tiny stapler that couldn't have been longer than her thumb. George's contained a bag of marbles, Jane's a puzzle game with a ball and a maze. Their included jokes were as lame as Reid's.

Tate's Christmas cracker held a small stuffed bear. One he stared at for an inordinately long time. His eyes tracked to his mother's, who blinked away tears as she shook her head.

"What a silly coincidence." She waved a hand but Hayden knew that symbol of a special moment between mother and son was anything but silly.

"Your turn," Tate told Hayden as she took the end of her cracker and he took the other. After the pop, a gaudy ring fell from her cracker. "Look at that. A matching set."

"Not quite. Mine's bigger than Reid's." Hayden eyed Tate's brother, trying to keep things light.

"Maybe you should see if it fits." Drew's winked, pure, adorable *evil*. Not at all interested in keeping the focus off Hayden's ring.

Hayden cast Tate an unsure look but he didn't waver. He took the ring from her hand and slid it onto her ring finger, admiring it in the candlelight.

The tacky plastic trinket shimmered, silver glitter swimming within the blue stone. It was gumball-machine quality, and completely ridiculous, but there was something symbolic about Tate slipping it onto her hand in front of his family that caused a lump to rise in her throat.

"The perfect placeholder while yours is being sized, then," Jane said, repeating the false story Hayden had given about why she wasn't wearing a ring.

"Right."

"My boys. Married and happy. It's all I ever wanted." Jane folded her hands at her chest and Hayden hoped it escaped notice that she and Tate were silent on the matter.

The only real part of their relationship was that she and Tate liked each other a whole hell of a lot.

"Your crown," Tate slipped the thin paper ring over Hayden's hair and, following tradition, she reached for her joke.

"Why does Santa have three gardens?" She waited a beat and then wrinkled her nose. "So he can 'ho ho ho.'" She groaned but everyone at the table erupted in laughter.

"Worst one yet." Tate leaned forward to kiss her. It occurred to her that he'd been careful about being affectionate with her in front of his family, and she him. Now he lingered over her lips, placing a second kiss there before murmuring, "Merry Christmas, Hayden."

"Jane wants us to delay our flight," Tate said as he packed away another sweater into his suitcase. They'd stayed downstairs after dinner, drinking and laughing and enjoying his their family's traditional Christmas pudding.

That brought discussion of more of his newfound family, which had led to photo albums. Turned out he had a lot of cousins, aunts, uncles and one living grand-father in the area.

"When you return, we'll have a visit," Jane had told him, hinting that she'd been careful not to overwhelm him this trip.

"It's Boxing Day tomorrow, which is a national holiday here," he continued telling Hayden, who sat on the bed. Things had gone well so far, but staying longer seemed to be pushing his luck. "They go to a restaurant and out shopping, and then there's a duck race with rubber duckies for charity in the afternoon." He raised his eyebrows. "I had no idea."

He'd booked their flights to be in and out quickly, figuring he'd be ready to retreat to the sanctity of Spright Island as soon as possible. But he wasn't as ready as he'd originally thought. He was enjoying his parents, Reid and Drew, and Hayden.

She still wore the ring he'd put on her finger at dinner. When Drew had suggested she try it on, Tate hadn't hesitated. Part of living dangerously included not over-thinking moments like that one. But he couldn't deny the part of him that wanted it to be real—as real as the family who, before this trip, had been no more than a story. Would bringing Hayden deeper into his life be the same as it'd been with the Singletons? At first a vague notion, and then 3D reality come to life… Did he *want* to be in deeper?

Discomfort bubbled in his gut, and the thought of "don't push your luck" occurred again. There was fun and then there was stupid, and he'd been walking that razor's edge.

"You should take that off before it turns your finger green."

Hayden gave her finger one lingering look before agreeing, "I guess you're right." She tugged the ring from her hand and set it on the night table next to the bed.

See? She doesn't want to go deeper either.

"With everything going on, I hadn't so much as thought about putting a real ring on your finger for show. I should've known everyone would expect it." Not that he'd have even considered giving her the one Claire had worn. That thing was a bad omen. He hadn't gotten around to selling it yet, but he would. Another act in the one-man play he was calling *Moving On.*

"You've had a lot on your mind." Hayden came to him and traced the lines bracketing his mouth. "This will become easier, Tate. You'll see. You'll get used to having extra family, and then you'll find a way to include them all into your big, amazing life."

"You always know what to say." Always knew how to put everything into instant perspective. His lips hovered dangerously close to hers. "Thank you for coming. I couldn't have done this without you."

He meant it. Considering the depth of the emotional pitfalls he'd experienced recently, he'd tackled them with relative ease. Hayden had his back, and he didn't take that lightly.

Hayden tilted her face, her lips brushing his. "I'm glad I could help." One eyebrow lifted impishly. "You owe me, Duncan."

He gave her bottom lip a gentle nip. "Will you take payment in sexual favors?"

"My favorite kind of currency."

He kissed her, his lips sliding over hers as he settled against her in bed. He lost himself in her plush mouth, the friction from her writhing hips into his crotch giving him a damn good idea.

Her soft moans urged him on, and Tate had them out of their clothes a short while later. He was suddenly very grateful he'd stopped in the rain outside her studio that night.

Grateful for her in any capacity, even a temporary one. Maybe they were only meant to be together through this particularly difficult part of his life. Maybe once the storms cleared and the sun shined, they'd be ready to move on.

Somehow, though, he doubted it.

He took his time kissing every inch of her he exposed. Every soft, muscular, firm yet giving bit of her, until her breaths were short and fast.

She stroked his jaw with cool fingertips as she murmured her praise. And he took his time, memorizing the details of her beneath him just in case their time together ended before he was ready.

Seventeen

"Are you sure you don't want to come along?" Tate asked his mother.

"You kids go on without us. I've had my fun."

After making love to Hayden last night, she'd convinced Tate to stay another day. She argued that she didn't have classes until after the new year, anyway, then added, "You're enjoying yourself. It'd be good for you." When he hesitated, she resorted to teasing him. "What's wrong? Can't afford to change our flight times?"

That had earned her a tickle fight that turned into slow, openmouthed kisses. When he tried to pull her under him again, she'd shoved him in the direction of his laptop. He'd reluctantly left the warm bed and made the necessary changes to their tickets.

"Listen to your mother," George warned now, beer

glass raised. They'd spent the Boxing Day in downtown London for the most part, shopping and visiting
a variety of booths in what was normally a concrete
jungle. From there they'd gone to a pub for a beer and
snacks, when Jane mentioned "you'd better see your-
selves to Hyde Park before it's too late."

"Yeah, listen to your mother," Reid echoed George.
"Look at her. A woman her age probably needs to rest
her weary bones."

Jane Singleton was nowhere near "weary." Her blue
eyes were bright and sparkling, her smile soft and easy.
No longer did she have that haunted look in her eyes
like she'd seen a ghost—though Tate reasoned that he
was a ghost in a way.

"She needs tea," Reid continued, not heeding the
warning glare from Jane. "And a nap."

"Careful, son, or you'll be wearing that drink,"
George warned with a chuckle. "The truth of the matter is we want the house to ourselves." He wrapped his
arms around his wife and kissed her neck while Jane
laughed and gave his arm a halfhearted swat.

Tate smiled at the display, grateful they'd had each
other while he was missing. Grateful that what had
happened to him hadn't torn apart their marriage.

"What do you think?" Tate asked Hayden, but he
could've guessed her thoughts given the size of her
grin.

"I'd be remiss to leave London without seeing a
light garden in Hyde Park." She turned to Jane. "And
I'd never rob you of an evening with your very handsome husband."

"Hear, hear," Drew said with enthusiasm, holding her club soda in the air.

"But take photos!" Jane requested. "Of the light garden, the observation wheel, roller coasters and, oh! Ice skating!"

"Do you ice skate, *darling*?" Hayden asked, her syrupy tone teasing.

"You've seen me move," Tate murmured into her ear before kissing her warm cheek. "What do you think?"

Reid, ever the encourager of public displays of affection, put his fingers between his lips and whistled.

London had been culture shock for Hayden since she arrived, so she was pleasantly surprised to find the winter wonderland event in Hyde Park was similar to what she'd come to expect of carnivals and fairs back home.

Well, aside from the aged, regal architecture she'd seen driving in, which had been preserved from another era entirely.

The park itself was overdone in the best way imaginable. Gaudy, blinking bulbs decorated every stall and stand, including on the huge lit entrance sign announcing "Winter Wonderland."

Entry was free, but there were opportunities to buy everything from food to shirts and jewelry to artwork. Bars dotted the park as well as venues for live shows, a funhouse, and a Ferris wheel—which must've been what Jane meant by "observation" wheel. The ice skating rink was *enormous*, children and adults alike moving across the slick surface with various stages of skill. Some gliding, others flailing.

Hayden would probably manage something between a glide and a flail if they ventured that direction.

Tate waggled their hands. They were connected by interlocked fingers and she'd gone without gloves given the mild weather. It was chilly, but not cold and while fog threatened, it hadn't brought rain.

"Since I can't have beer, I insist upon sugar," Drew announced, pointing at a stall with candy bins filled with lollipops, candy necklaces and gummy everything.

"Done. Should we meet up at the light garden?" Reid asked.

"Yeah, one hour. We're going to try to skate," Tate called to his brother. Reid nodded his acknowledgment.

Tate, bracketing Hayden's hips with his hands, pulled her ass against his crotch. "Let's see what you're made of, gorgeous."

Snow machines blew flaked ice into the air as they laced up, Hayden unsure what she was getting herself into.

"I'm sure it's like riding a bike," she'd famously said before falling onto her backside. They made their way clumsily around the rink once, and by round two, while they hadn't exactly glided, they had swept across the ice in a way that was at least semicompetent.

Skates off, boots on, she and Tate made their way to the closest booth that sold beverages and sat on a nearby bench with their drinks.

"Thank God for my core strength," she said with a laugh over her paper cup of wassail.

"I enjoyed watching you wobbling across the ice."

She nudged him, careful not to spill his drink into

his lap. "You actually did better than me. I'm impressed." She poked him in the belly, and his abdomen clenched into a wall of muscle beneath her finger. Which reminded her of what he looked like without any clothes, and that in turn reminded her of what they did together best. "It's kind of a turn-on."

"Ice skating turns you on?" Tate lifted a dubious eyebrow.

"Pretty sure you doing anything turn me on." She said it with an almost disappointed lilt. This fantasy of being fake engaged, the fairy tale of Christmas in London, was about to come to an end. She'd been tempering her reactions, trying to monitor the way she responded to him, but she wasn't always able to keep her true feelings from surfacing.

She issued a reminder that it was smart not to grow accustomed to flying business class to London at Christmas, or having a Hallmark-style scene on ice skates...

Hayden had become independent out of necessity. Since the moment she'd invited Tate into her apartment—into her *life*—he'd been chipping away at the wall she safely hid behind. She felt a pull toward him that was simply undeniable.

"I could say the same to you, Ms. Green." She was rewarded with a kiss that reminded her of the wassail. Sweet, clovey, cinnamony...*temporary*.

"You freak me out a little," she admitted. "I'm not used to...so much lavish treatment."

"Excuse me? Lavish? We hopped on a plane. We're at a park."

"You flew us to London in our own private pods!

We're at *Hyde Park*. You own an entire community, meanwhile I'm leasing my studio and my apartment."

"And my treating you to what you deserve is making you uncomfortable?"

"I…" But her pending argument died on her tongue. She was stuck on the "deserve" part. Tate had no problem filling the silence.

"You do deserve it, Hayden. The good life. It's not reserved to people who were lucky enough to be born into it. Or adopted into it," he added softly.

"My grandmother's an alcoholic," she blurted out, as if the secret of her own parentage refused to be stuffed down any longer. "And my mother is a master of guilt. Both at absorbing it and doling it out."

Tate's eyebrows knitted, but he stayed quiet. She hadn't opened up to him about just how wide the gap was between his life and hers, and it seemed wrong not to share at this point. She knew his secrets.

"When I moved out on my own for the first time, they didn't let a day go by without reminding me that I was betraying them in the worst way possible. And when I moved to the refuge of Spright Island, they were jealous. Enormously jealous." She rolled her eyes as she replayed her mother's words about Hayden being *too good for them*. "I saved and saved and saved. And I work hard. I earned the right to live there. I made that decision on my own. It didn't come without a price, though. I'm not sure I have what I deserve."

She smiled sadly as she remembered another conversation with her mom, this one before she left for London. Patti Green hadn't been supportive of her daughter choosing to "flit around the globe" over spending time with family.

"Sometimes the healthiest choice for you isn't the popular one," Tate said. "I love my adoptive parents but when I found out about the Singletons visiting them became hard. I drew boundary lines around them even though I knew it would hurt my mother's feelings."

She heaved a sigh. "Adulting is hard."

"The worst," he agreed, but his smile was light, and she felt the weight lift from her shoulders having admitted some family conflict of her own.

"After the new year, life will return to normal," she reminded both of them. "But getting lost in this—" she gestured to the gazebo with a decorated tree in the center and the many, many ropes of lights strung in every direction "—is worth it."

"Good."

"Thank you, Tate. I really appreciate you—this. You've been generous."

"Stop making this sound like goodbye." A little lean forward would be all it took to kiss him. A tiny nudge all it would take for him to mean so, so much more to her.

But it was Christmastime, and Tate smelled like wassail and leather, so Hayden lost herself in the heat of his mouth, and postponed worrying about the consequences for a little while longer.

Eighteen

Recovering from jet lag took a lot longer than Hayden anticipated.

The flight back from London was unremarkable and a lot less comfortable than the flight there. Despite Tate's insistence they change airlines to book first class or charter a private jet to go home, Hayden refused. She'd assured him that any seat was fine. He'd finally let her convince him and they'd ended up crammed in a middle aisle in a tight seat for the incredibly long flight home.

She'd needed the reminder that life wasn't all champagne and caviar. Halfway through the flight, however, as she was trying to stretch in the pitiful space between her seat and the one in front of her she realized she was being ridiculous. Why was it so hard for her to indulge?

As part of her new year's resolutions next year, she

was just going to enjoy her damn self. Tate had been a good sport, sending her a weary "I told you so" glance, but never bothering with the sentiment. She'd ended up apologizing once they were back in SWC, but he'd only kissed her forehead and sent her up to her apartment before returning home himself.

Now that she'd been home for a few days and was well rested, she was having what might be the most productive day of her life. She'd finished her laundry, planned her meals for the week, *and* finalized her class schedule for January as well as posting it on her website.

A knock at her door came earlier than she expected. Tate had made dinner plans for them to eat at the Brass Pony. She was wearing one of two new dresses she'd purchased since she'd returned home. One in black for the New Year's Eve party, which was much fancier than the red one she wore now.

"You weren't supposed to be here until six," she said as she pulled open the door. He was dressed handsomely in a suit sans tie, the collar open on a crisp white shirt. But his face was drawn, his mouth downturned.

"Wow. Rough day?"

"You could say that." He handed her a tall white cup from EterniTea. "They haven't opened yet, but I know a guy. Thought you might like to try the green tea latte."

"Thanks."

He leaned in and kissed her, lingering over her lips as he pulled in a breath. "Ready to go?"

"Are you sure you *want* to go?"

"Of course." He made a half-assed attempt at a smile but it didn't reach his eyes.

"Do you want to talk about it?" The second she asked her phone beeped—her mother's ringtone, which was as dooming as Darth Vader's theme song.

She staunchly ignored it, sipping her tea instead. "This is delicious."

"Don't you want to get that?" He frowned.

"No." Hayden had tried to call her mother to let her know she'd returned from London. She hadn't heard back and had counted herself lucky. "It's my mom."

"We have time."

"Trust me. Answering that call isn't about *time*. My family's…not like yours."

"British?" he teased.

"Normal."

"No family is normal. Answer it. If you do and find it's more drama with no real point, then mention we are headed to dinner and hang up. It's just that easy."

"And if it's an actual emergency?"

"Then we'll deal with it."

We.

She realized upon hearing that word that she'd never had support when it came to her family. It'd always been more of an "us versus them" situation.

"I'm sure your day was rough enough without dealing with—" the phone beeped again "—whatever this is."

Tate remained resolutely silent, even when the chime of her voice mail sounded.

"Fine," she told him, lifting her cell phone and turning on the speaker. "Here we go."

The recording started with a frantic "Oh, Hayden" that chilled her blood. Hayden's mother spoke between nervous breaths.

"Your grandmother is in the ER." Her mother's recorded voice shook. "This is worse than usual, Hayden. Much worse." Patti went on dispensing one horrific detail after the last, which made Hayden worry all the more. Patti ended the call with the name of the hospital.

Hayden crossed the living room to grab her keys and purse but was confronted by Tate, who plucked the keys from her hand.

"I'll drive."

Her head was already shaking. "I can't ask you to do that."

"You didn't ask. I told you we'd deal with it. Let's deal with it."

After years of independence and relying on herself, Tate, even after hearing that voice mail, was willing to go with her. It was hard to accept.

"Yes, but…"

"You met my family."

As if that was the same? But then she thought about how he'd been brave enough to ask for her help. Was she brave enough to accept his?

"Hayden." He held her hand. That was all it took to convince her. She let him lead her to the door and the uncertainty that waited for them at Seattle Memorial Hospital.

A hard, bitter line was the best description of Hayden's mouth as she navigated the hospital's hallways. She was a woman on a mission, and reminded

Tate more of a woman who was walking into a courtroom to hear a verdict than someone visiting her sick grandmother.

He'd dealt with his own bullshit today in the form of Casey Huxley. Tate had spent an hour arguing with the jackass head contractor who was spearheading the new neighborhood in SWC—that "secret" project model Hayden had stumbled upon in Tate's upstairs bedroom.

Casey had been amenable to the design until recently. Now they were arguing over bulldozing more trees to expand. It wasn't happening. Tate wouldn't compromise nature simply because Casey was too lazy to find a workaround.

At the nurse's desk, they learned that Hayden's grandmother had been downgraded from ICU to a room of her own, which only firmed the bitter line of Hayden's lips, causing them to vanish altogether.

He didn't have a lot of experience with true dysfunction and had zero experience with alcoholism, but he knew stressful situations which was clearly what she was involved in here.

"When's the last time you took a deep breath?" he asked, catching her wrist before she could march in the direction of her grandmother's room.

Hayden glared up at him, unwilling to let go and let God.

"Wouldn't it be better to walk into that room calm and collected?" he tried again. Advice he could've taken from himself earlier when he'd been in a screaming match with Casey in the trailer at the worksite. Tate would have some backpedaling to do if he hoped to quell the gossip train. Destroying land was a hot button for him. He refused to compromise his integrity, or his island's.

She didn't look happy about it, but Hayden took one breath, then another. "You don't have to go in with me. My family is… They're…" She shook her head, giving up.

"Family," he answered. "Not serial killers. Family. Messy, complicated, unpredictable."

"The student becomes the teacher." Her smile was faint.

"I'm a fast learner."

In the hospital room, there was an empty bed by the door and a frail, pale woman in a bed by the window. He guessed the woman at her side holding her hand to be Hayden's mother. She had the same dark brown hair, but shot through with gray. She carried more weight than Hayden and her face was lined.

A man in jeans and a long-sleeved sweater approached from the corridor, limping like he had a bum knee. He didn't seem very old, but his beer belly and the dark circles beneath his eyes aged him.

"Hayd. You made it." His voice was bright, almost cheery. Odd considering the situation.

"Hi, Dad." Hayden's smile was cautious as she held herself in check. No warm family greetings here.

"Went to grab a coffee. Guess we'll be here awhile." He sipped from his cup before turning to Tate. "Hello."

"Dad, this is Tate Duncan. He drove me here. Tate, my father, Glenn."

"Nice to see you, Tate. Can I grab either of you a cup of coffee?"

"No, thank you," Hayden told him.

Tate tried not to take her "he drove me here" comment personally, as if he was a chauffer and not the man who'd taken her to London over the holidays.

"Okey-doke. Well, I'll let you go in and visit, then. I'll wander around." In place of goodbye, he said, "Tate," and then turned and walked away from them.

"He's mellow." It might've been the strangest interaction Tate had ever had with a parent, and that was saying something.

"It's a coping mechanism," she said.

"Hayden? Oh, Hayden!" Her mother, having just noticed them at the threshold, frantically waved her deeper into the room. Hayden's grandmother lifted her head, her eyelids narrowing. Tate could've sworn the temperature of the room went down a few degrees.

"Hi, Mom." Hayden gave her mother a side hug and then dipped her chin to acknowledge her grandmother. "Grandma Winnie. How are you feeling?"

"Welllll, if it isn't the princess from the high tower," came Winnie's barbed reply, her voice dripping with sarcasm. "So nice of you to deign to come visit us common folk." She turned stony eyes on Tate and barked, "Who the hell are you?"

Nineteen

Here we go.

Hayden shot Tate an apologetic smile, feeling instantly guilty that she hadn't warned him. Anyone she'd dated as an adult had no reason to meet *the fam*, and the guys she dated when she was living at home weren't exactly the kinds of guys to bring home to mom.

"Mother, your heart," Patti warned Winnie.

"Don't worry about my heart," Winnie snapped. "Worry about smuggling in a cocktail. It's long past five o'clock. Keeping an old woman from one of her only pleasures in life is criminal."

What's her other pleasure in life? Bossing around my mother? Hayden wisely kept the snide thought to herself.

"Well?" Winnie speared Tate with a glare. "Introduce yourself."

"Tate Duncan," he replied coolly, hands tucked into his pants pockets. "I'm also Wesley Singleton, but that's a long, complicated story."

Hayden gaped at him before turning back to her grandmother.

"Never heard of you." Winnie's frown pulled the corners of her mouth lower.

Hayden looked up to tell Tate they could leave—no one should be subjected to her grandmother's abuse, but he chuckled good-naturedly.

"I'm not surprised," he said. "My reality show airs late at night, and I keep my celebrity appearances to a minimum."

"Smart-ass." But Winnie's mouth curled at the edge. Was it possible that Tate was winning over the world's biggest critic? It'd been a long while since Hayden's grandmother had regarded anyone with respect, so the experience was unique.

Patti, meanwhile, didn't catch the joke. "You have a reality television show?"

"Not yet," Tate's smile remained. Amazing.

Hayden gestured toward the hallway. "Can I talk to you in private, Mom?"

"What's wrong with in here?" Winnie demanded.

"Nothing's wrong, ma'am," Tate answered for them.

"Ma'am," Winnie barked, amused.

Had Hayden ever heard that sound come from her most embittered family member?

"I'll be right back, Mother," Patti told Winnie as she walked for the corridor. Winnie's call of "and bring me a cocktail on your way back!" followed her out and then the volume on the television skyrocketed.

"She's really very sweet," Hayden's mother explained to Tate once they were outside of the room.

Hayden barely banked an eye roll.

"No judgment from me," he said easily. When Hayden looked up at him she was surprised to see the sincerity on his face. He meant it. He wasn't standing in judgment of her or her family tonight.

Hand around her waist, he tucked her close, and Patti didn't miss it.

"You two seem close. Hayden and I used to be that close." She sent a woe-is-me look at her only daughter. "I'm glad for her though."

Hayden hated that she was skeptical, but her mother had accused her of "flitting" to London instead of spending time with her family.

"Are you the one who took her to London?"

"Mom—"

"Yes. To meet my birth parents."

"Oh." Patti's ears pricked at the barest whiff of gossip. But then she faced Hayden, guns blazing. "You met his parents. And *this* is how you choose to introduce him to us?"

"That's not… We're not…" Hayden closed her eyes and pulled in another deep breath, staunching her knee-jerk reaction. She didn't owe Patti an explanation about why she did anything. "Why is she really here, Mom?"

"What's that supposed to mean?"

"It means you should look into rehab if Grandma Winnie's drinking so much she's blacking out."

"Blacking out? Who told you that?" Patti's eyes widened, flicking to Tate first as she offered a shaky smile of embarrassment. "This is hardly the place to air family grievances, Hayden. Your grandmother is ill."

"Yes, very." Hayden couldn't help agreeing. "She has been sick with this illness for as long as I can remember. You can't stop her. I can't stop her. I came as a courtesy…"

"A courtesy!" Patti let out a sharp, humorless laugh. "Well, my, my. Excuse us for interrupting your glamorous life. By all means, go and enjoy a *fabulous* night with your *celebrity* boyfriend. If you'll excuse me." She saved one last disingenuous smile for Tate before stomping back into the hospital room.

Drained and exhausted from that brief interaction, Hayden shook her head at Tate, at a loss for what to say.

He suffered no such loss.

"I don't remember if I told you…" His arm still looped at her waist, he walked with her toward the exit. "You couldn't look more beautiful if you tried. I like you in red."

She shook her head. He was too much.

"Did you also know that your *celebrity boyfriend* knows the chef at the Brass Pony personally?"

"I did not." She was grinning, a feat in and of itself.

"It's true. Any special requests you have for your *glamorous* dinner are well within reach."

Warm browns, golds, and greens made up the décor at the Brass Pony, along with gilded frames holding mirrors and paintings of horses and landscapes. The tables were lit by low candles on crisp, white tablecloths, the silverware was gold and the glassware copious.

Upon entering, Hayden took her first full breath in

hours, embarrassed more by her own behavior than her family's. What must Tate think of her? That she's completely intolerant?

"Mr. Duncan." A man in a smart blue suit, his hair dusky blond, regarded Tate with both surprise what could've been a borderline nervous smile. "I haven't seen you in a while."

"Jared." Tate's hand on her back, he ushered her forward, then offered that hand in greeting to the manager of the Pony. "Apologies for my behavior last time I was in here. You caught me on one of my worst days. This is Hayden Green, she owns the yoga studio down the street."

"A pleasure, Hayden." Jared nodded his greeting then said to Tate, "Glad to have you back. Your usual table?"

"If it's available."

"Right this way."

Hayden had been to the Brass Pony once since she moved here. The food was exquisite; the atmosphere on the stuffy side, but it had its merits. For one, it was quiet. It was also tidy. Bussers, waitstaff and hosts were dressed in black pants, long black aprons and white shirts with the restaurant's green logo on them.

Tate's "usual table" was located in a back corner, the C-shaped booth tall and private. From her spot in the center of the C, the restaurant's patrons were visible, but Hayden and Tate were shielded from prying eyes.

In short order they were served a bottle of wine, goblets of water and a special made by the chef that Tate requested.

All part of dating a billionaire, Hayden thought with a wry smile.

Fiddling with her gold fork, Hayden tried to think of a way to explain her behavior tonight. Explain that she'd endured years and years of neglect and verbal abuse from her grandmother and mother. Explain that while Hayden loved them, they were complicated to know and even more complicated to like.

Before she could arrive at any arrangement of those words, though, Tate spoke.

"My parents—the Duncans—aren't perfect, either, you know." His blue eyes sparkled in the candlelight.

"Yes, but are they manipulative?"

"They can be." He lifted his wine. "They're parents."

"I don't want you think that I'm this uncaring, selfish—"

He reached for her hand, shaking his head to stay her words. "Don't. You already know what I think about you."

Did she? He must've seen the question on her face.

"Giving. Caring. Selfless. Beautiful. Strong. Patient. Enduring. Really, *really* amazing in bed." He grinned and she pulled her hand away to shove his arm.

"Do you see where we are? Behave yourself."

"I'm tired of behaving myself. You should know that better than anyone."

"Are you a rule breaker now?" she teased.

"More like the rules I put stock into were broken for me. I'm enjoying not heeding them. And so should you."

She sipped her wine, both rich and complex, like the man who ordered it. "I'm not heeding any rules."

Not her mother's rule that Hayden should be involved in every family emergency. Not her own warning her not to get serious with a guy, or allow herself to be spoiled unnecessarily. And dining "off" the menu and letting her date treat her to a trip to another country definitely counted as her being spoiled.

No, she wasn't following any rules, which she knew damn well could lead to breaking even more of them. But as she met Tate's eyes over their appetizer of crisp calamari, she couldn't dredge up any motivation to change.

Although…maybe he'd changed her already.

Twenty

Hayden had dreamed of attending the swanky New Year's Eve party in SWC since she moved here.

As a business owner, she'd received a coveted vellum invitation to the event last year. Knee-deep in doing two million things business owners *without personal assistants* did during the week of Christmas, she hadn't been able to attend. By the time last year's party rolled around, she was full-on Cinderella minus the Fairy Godmother. She'd been overworked, exhausted, and in need of a mani, pedi, haircut *and* eyebrow wax. Readying herself for a fancy party where she'd be expected to present her best self was as far-off a fantasy as waiting for a prince to knock on her door with a glass slipper on a silk pillow.

So. She'd stayed home.

The FOMO had been epic.

This year, though, she was going. She had an invitation in hand, a gorgeous date chauffeuring her to the event, and a dress she'd picked up on the clearance rack of Basic Black Boutique in town. The dress was black and low-cut in the front, formfitting to show her curves, and sparkled no matter which way she turned thanks to a zillion small silver "diamonds" sewn into the fabric. She'd swept her hair up for the night and pulled on a silver cuff bracelet and chandelier earrings, forgoing the necklace. The plunging neckline drew enough attention without one.

Tate had offered to buy her a gown for tonight, but she'd declined. After the night of the hospital drama, he'd been everything she needed, and she didn't feel right expecting more. He'd taken her to the Brass Pony—where they ate an incredible gourmet meal that wasn't on the menu—and he didn't ask her to explain or talk about it. She'd opted to do neither. For too long her mother and grandmother had dictated her moods. Being in that hospital had cemented the reason she'd left Seattle in the first place: She wanted be her own woman—independent and self-reliant. And yes, that, too, was part of the driving force that led her to buying her own dress.

Excited, she waited in her yoga studio rather than outside, watching out the wide windows for Tate's Mercedes to show. She'd insisted on meeting him there, but he wouldn't allow it, even though the event was closer to his house than hers. It seemed no matter how much distance she tried to put between them he closed the gap.

She fingered the lacy material of her shoulder wrap

as she paced along the scuffed studio floor. She'd shown up for him in London, and he'd shown up for her at the hospital. Originally she'd believed it was tit for tat, a simple exchange of favors. But that wasn't all this was, was it?

She'd erected that independence wall, building it as tall as she could. Ever since she'd said yes to Tate, he'd been chipping away at it and now that wall was crumbling. Through the holes she was seeing a future she'd never imagined.

Tate was in that future.

Not temporarily, not as means to goods and services, or favors. He was there, bold and exciting, for one simple reason.

She'd fallen for him.

Like Buttercup for Westley in *The Princess Bride*, Hayden had tumbled ass over teakettle down the hill, with her heart bouncing ahead of her.

Not her brightest move to date, but what was she supposed to do about it? Tate was giving, and kind, and great in bed and hot—*don't forget hot*. Puttying in the holes in that crumbling wall of hers was no longer an option. What used to be her protection was now starting to resemble a prison. She didn't *want* to hide behind a wall any longer.

Her ride pulled to the curb, and she drew her wrap over her shoulders and stepped outside. Gripping her clutch, she shuddered as sharp, icy wind cut through the thin garment. Nevertheless, she'd worn a sleeveless dress and had slipped her feet into sparkly peep-toe black heels to show off her new pedicure. No detail went unnoticed when she readied herself for tonight.

It wasn't every day she told the man of her dreams she'd fallen for him.

Stupid? Maybe. She had no idea how he'd react. But she couldn't think of a better time than midnight on New Year's Eve to tell him. That would blow up her wall completely.

Tate stepped out of the car in a black tuxedo and bow tie that weakened her knees. How…*how* could this man look good in literally any style of clothing?

He stopped short of opening her door for her, his eyes roaming over her dress, his mouth slightly open like he was going to say something but forgot what it was.

"I guess you can 'buy your own damn dress,'" he joked, throwing her words back to her. She hadn't been angry when she said it, just exasperated. She wouldn't allow him to cater to her *constantly*.

"I couldn't figure out how else to make you stop offering." She grinned.

"Fair enough." He opened her door and she walked to him, tall enough in her heels to place a cold kiss on his warm mouth. He swatted her ass, reminding her that as gentlemanly as he was, he couldn't be defined him by only that word.

He was much more layered, and meant more to her than she'd previously imagined. All because she'd met him outside in the rain and offered him a cup of tea.

The Common, a rentable space for parties and where SWC held most of their meetings and sponsored parties, was a sea of Edison lights dangling from the ceiling.

Hayden couldn't suppress a gasp when she stepped

through the double doors and was met with those glowing bulbs hanging from black wires and tied with a lush black bow at the base.

"Tate." She clutched the arm of his tuxedo, admiring the many guests in their finery. The black tie affair was dripping with luxury, from the gold and black and white decorations to the five-piece jazz band playing softly onstage.

The fairy tale, it seemed, was real.

"I like that smile." He brushed her lips with his. "Don't want to ruin your lipstick."

"Ruin away. I have more."

As they walked through the room, the guests parted like the Red Sea for Moses. All eyes were on Tate. In this community, he really was a celebrity.

He shook a few hands and introduced her to a few new people, though she spotted a lot of people she knew, too. She might not be as iconic as the *great and powerful Tate Duncan*, but seeing so many familiar faces reminded her that she'd built a life here as well.

She released Tate's arm to accept the glass of champagne, and he raised his own.

"To your first NYE at SWC." They *cheersed* and sipped, and wow, even the champagne was expensive. Tate wouldn't have had it any other way.

"This is incredible. I feel like Cinderella."

"Good." Arm locked around her waist, he leaned in to kiss her, pausing a breath from her lips to mutter a very unromantic *"Son of a bitch."*

"Duncan." The gruff voice belonged to guy nearly seven feet tall, with arms the size of 55-gallon drums. His hair was buzzed close to his head, his mustache thick and walrus-like. He turned stony eyes to Hayden for a brief moment before glaring at Tate.

"Hayden Green," Tate said after a long, and awkward, pause. "Casey Huxley. I've mentioned him before. The contractor partnering with me to build a group of houses on the eastern side of the island."

"Oh. *Oh.*" The top-secret project that wasn't really secret, she remembered. Also, she'd learned at their dinner at the Brass Pony, the same contractor who Tate had argued with over taking down quite a few trees in SWC.

She hadn't wanted to talk about her drama, but she'd needled Tate about his. He'd shared, and she let him, until it was obvious from his copious swearing she shouldn't have pried.

She had hoped Tate and Casey would work out their differences. Since they stood positioned like they were about to have Wild West style shoot-out, it was safe to assume that hadn't happened yet.

Casey took a champagne flute, delicate in his wide, meaty palm, and with a final eye slice to Tate, stalked off in the opposite direction.

"That was intense," she told Tate after Casey was out of earshot. "The way you made it sound, you two nearly went to fisticuffs the other day."

"Nearly," he grated, then, "Don't look so concerned. I can take him."

"I wasn't thinking that." She palmed the front of his tux and smoothed her hands over his built chest. He wasn't a slouch by anyone's definition. "I was hoping you two would have worked things out."

"He cares about control, I care about my island. We're nowhere near being on the same page."

"Tate!" A cheery man with dark olive skin, dark hair approached.

"Terry Guerrero." Tate pumped the other man's hand and then introduced Hayden.

"Nice to meet you." Terry's accent hinted at Spanish descent. He was so friendly it was almost jarring after the tense run-in with Casey.

"I promised Terry I'd talk to him about the development tonight, but that was before I made plans with you." Tate narrowed his eyes jovially at Terry. "I'm guessing you're holding me to it."

"Much as I hate to sully your evening with business, I'm going to on vacation tomorrow for two weeks. I'm not working from the Bahamas—Ana would kill me."

"Good man," Tate said.

"I'll have to introduce you to my wife," Terry told Hayden, "when she's finished chatting up the interior designer—the woman who designed this party. What is her name? No doubt Ana wants to hit her up to do our daughter's engagement party."

"Lois Sherwood," Tate answered. "And congratulations."

Hayden knew Lois. The chatty gray-haired woman was waving her arms in the air, excitement reigning supreme as she spoke with Terry's wife. She was an energetic, busy little thing. And flexible. Lois attended yoga classes three times a week.

Tate and Terry spoke for another minute before Terry excused himself. "I'll be at the bar. Hayden, a pleasure."

Once he was gone, Tate let out a sigh.

"Go. I should probably be hobnobbing with business folk, too. This event is meant to bring business owners together after all, right?" She smiled, quoting the wording on the invitation.

"I guess." His mouth quirked playfully before he leaned in to kiss her. He didn't make it this time, either. Sherry interrupted next.

"Look at you two! You two are the cutest ever!" Sherry shuffled in place like she couldn't contain her joy, but lowered her voice conspiratorially when she spoke again. "I knew it! I knew it! Even in that class we took together, I *knew* Tate had a thing for you."

Hayden stole a glance up at Tate to find him wearing a patient smile.

"Your timing is perfect," Hayden told the other woman. "Tate was about to talk business at the bar and leave me standing here alone. Should we grab you a refill?"

Sherry glanced down at her empty glass. "Oh, goodness. Must be a hole in my glass. I'll grab another and meet you right back here." She pointed at Tate and then Hayden before moving to the nearest waiter to pluck a flute from a tray.

"I see her caffeine addiction hasn't gone anywhere," he muttered.

"*You're welcome* for letting you off the hook."

"I'll be brief," he promised.

"You'd better." Hayden gripped his lapels and kissed him solidly before someone else came along to interrupt.

After he met with Terry to discuss the new SWC neighborhood, Tate spotted Hayden in a conversation with a cluster of women. He decided to hang back and give her time to work her magic. By the delighted smile on her face he could tell she was enjoying her first SWC New Year's gala.

He watched her a beat longer, wondering if he'd have noticed her if she'd come to last year's soiree. Yes. He would have. Even if she hadn't worn the sparkling black dress—an absolute showstopper. Her lethal curves and dark hair, full mouth and elegant way she handled herself in a pair of tall shoes would have been impossible to overlook.

She *glowed* with life.

Then again, he'd had a girlfriend last year at this time, so noticing Hayden would have been moot. He couldn't have acted on any passing attraction no matter how tempting she would've been.

He polished off his drink and relinquished the empty glass to the bar. Shoving his hands in his pockets, he strolled along the back of the room only to freeze in place a moment later when he spotted a familiar golden-haired, slim woman on the arm of Casey Huxley.

What the hell? Had he summoned her with his mind? And what was she doing attached to Casey, of all people? Especially now that the bigger man had cemented himself into the role of Tate's nemesis.

How had Claire and Casey ended up in the same *room* together let alone found anything in common once they were there?

It was definitely his ex-fiancée, though. There was no mistaking her slightly upturned nose and the rigid way she held her shoulders. As if she felt eyes on her, she turned to face Tate fully, giving him a demure finger wave before standing on tiptoes to whisper into Casey's ear.

Casey murmured something to her, his coal black eyes on Tate. And then they parted, Claire heading unmistakably in Tate's direction.

Son of a bitch.

Twenty-One

Tate, with no other choice than to acknowledge Claire, crossed the distance to meet her halfway. Casey continued staring, but he wasn't Tate's problem tonight, or ever after Tate ended this deal.

"Hi, Tate." Claire stood before him, poised, wearing a no-nonsense black dress. No glitter, no shine, no light. Nothing like Hayden. The only sparkles on Claire were coming from the ring on her—

What the hell?

"Is that…" He hadn't meant to react, but there was no ignoring the giant diamond ring…on her left hand. She'd returned his engagement ring and, then what, run out to get engaged? *To Casey?*

She glanced down at her finger, almost like she'd forgotten the ring was there. "Oh, yes. I'm engaged."

"To Casey Huxley?"

"What? No. God, no. We're business partners, Casey and I. He invited me as his plus-one to introduce me around. *We're* not engaged. I'm engaged to… someone else."

That was a lot to ingest. Tate didn't know what to ask about first. He'd offered to introduce Claire around plenty when they'd dated, but she never would come with him anywhere. He'd start there.

"You hate Spright Island."

"As a residence, yes. As a business opportunity, no."

"Since when are you interested in land development?"

"Guess you rubbed off on me." She tipped her head. "It's my new side gig."

Tate's livelihood—no, *life's purpose*—was Claire's *side gig*? He was certain anger was turning his face a deep shade of pink.

"Are you getting back at me for something?" It was the only explanation that made sense. That or he was having his own private *Twilight Zone* moment.

"Always about you, isn't it Tate?" She rolled her eyes. "You're not the only one who knows what people want."

He had to let out a dry laugh at that. "And you do?"

"Casey and I do. People want wide open spaces. Room for lawns and yards. Fences."

"Suburbia." Tate's lip curled.

"People want lawns to mow, Tate."

The neighborhoods at SWC were designed to look as if they were tucked into the trees. There were no "lawns." Each plot fostered native vegetation—low growing plants interspersed with rocks and mulch. "I'd never compromise SWC's unique design. You know that. After our last meeting, Casey sure as hell knows that."

"People don't want to be buried in the woods."

"What the hell would you know about mowing a lawn or the woods? Aren't you a self-proclaimed city girl?"

"I like my space."

"No kidding." She'd taken plenty of it when it came to him. "You made it clear you didn't want to be married," he said through clenched teeth. Hayden hadn't noticed him missing yet. Maybe he could get her out of here before she laid eyes on Claire. He didn't want Hayden's evening to be ruined, too.

"Your family...confusion wasn't what I signed up for." Tate opened his mouth to say it wasn't what he'd signed up for, either, but before he could, Claire added, "I saw you with her earlier. Your date. She's—"

"Amazing," he interrupted, unwilling to let his ex-fiancée fill in the adjective. "*Amazing* is the word you're looking for, and even if it isn't, you can spare me your opinion."

His voice was hollow.

Like his chest.

Running into Claire had stolen the oxygen from his lungs and robbed him of reason. Probably there were some unexamined emotions revolving around their breakup he hadn't dealt with, but when would he have had the time?

Between winter holidays, and recovering from being in a couple, to trying to reacquaint himself with his brother and then Hayden... There hadn't been time to process much of anything. His head felt like a knotted ball of Christmas lights.

"Did you meet *him*—" Tate gestured to her engagement ring "—before or after ending it with me?"

Her mouth opened, then closed, but she didn't answer. At least she had the decency not to lie to him.

"Jesus, Claire."

"Don't judge me."

He took a deep breath and willed himself to stay calm. The last thing he needed was to make a scene and have this unfortunate run-in with his ex go down in the annals of Spright Wellness Community history.

"When you know you know." She offered a shrug. More platitudes.

"Listen, I don't want to fight." She held up a hand, calling a stop to the conversation he should've called quits to first. "I came over to say hello, and I wanted to come clean about my involvement in the new project. Personally, and before someone else told you."

"How magnanimous of you."

Her expression was sharp, unfriendly. "I'll keep my distance for the rest of the party. Casey's not interested in talking business tonight, anyway."

"What business? Casey's fired. Especially if you're involved in the design." So much for being the better person, but he couldn't help himself. He'd been ready to throw Casey off his island after that last meeting, but learning of Claire's involvement had sealed the other man's fate.

"Don't make threats. He won't refund your *very* large deposit, some of which was my seed money."

"Keep it," he grated, hating that he'd unknowingly

accepted money from Claire. Hating that he'd thought Casey might eventually come around to Tate's way of thinking.

With a shake of her blond head, she started back to the party.

"Who's the lucky guy?" he called after her.

"You don't know him." She blew him a kiss on her way out.

Thank God for small favors.

A blur of black caught Hayden's attention as she was resting her empty glass on a nearby tray. Tate's shoulders were beneath his ears, his fists balled at his sides.

He looked furious. Until she caught his eye and then he smiled, though it was a touch disingenuous.

"There you are." A few beads of sweat had broken out on his forehead.

"What happened to you?" She turned her head in the direction he'd come from but he pulled her close, one hand pressing her lower back, his other hand cradling her jaw. He gave her a lengthy kiss and she wobbled from the force of it, practically melting into him. Tate was an exceptional kisser.

"Wow, thank you," she said when he pulled away. He brushed her cheek with his thumb. "Was it that Neanderthal, Casey?"

He gave her a jerky nod.

"What did he do?" She searched the party, having half a mind to walk over to the idiot and give him a piece of her mind.

"He left." Tate turned Hayden's chin to face him. "Can we get out of here?"

She understood he was angry and processing an obviously loaded conversation, but... "Before midnight? I wanted to stay for the countdown."

She'd planned for a kiss at midnight under the chandelier in her beautiful dress. She'd planned on telling him she loved him.

"It's a lot to ask, I know." His frown faded, his lips softening some. "I have something better to do tonight."

Anticipation like warm honey trickled down her spine.

"You." He nuzzled her nose, charm dialed to eleven. "Ever since I saw you wearing that dress, I've been preoccupied with the idea of taking you out of it." His voice was a low murmur of appreciation, the flattery gaining him a lot of ground. She'd never been able to resist him when he couldn't resist her.

"Champagne at midnight here is special, but I have champagne at my house." He leaned close, his warm breath tickling her ear, his voice wickedly sexy. "When the clock strikes midnight, I'll drench you in champagne and kiss you everywhere the bubbles touch. Come home with me, Hayden, you won't regret it."

"That...is a compelling argument, Mr. Duncan," she practically purred. Tate offering private kisses at the stroke of midnight was more tempting than champagne toasts on New Year's, but she'd dreamed of counting down, kissing him, and offering up an *I love you*. "Can't we go home after? Midnight is a little over an hour away and—"

Blue eyes drilled into her. "It would mean *the world* to me if you and I could ring in the New Year alone."

Tonight she had very special plans for announcing how she felt about Tate, and by the look in his eyes, he had a similar announcement in mind. That was worth skipping the toast at the party. That was worth skipping a lifetime of toasts.

"Okay."

"Yeah?" He looked relieved as he cast another quick, maybe even nervous glance around.

"Yes. I'd love to go home with you."

His grin was heady and gorgeous, the attractive smile lines around his mouth and at the corners of his eyes in full force. She loved seeing him happy. She loved making him happy. Who cared about a silly toast when they had memories to make?

"Shall we?" He offered his arm, his relaxed features showing no signs of the turmoil she thought she'd seen earlier. Business rarely mixed with pleasure, but she was glad he hadn't allowed it to put a damper on the evening ahead of them. Not when he had so many delicious things in store for her.

"We shall," she said and then threaded her arm into his.

Twenty-Two

Flames in the gas fireplace bloomed to life and Tate tossed the remote onto the coffee table. Exactly how quickly he could turn her on, Hayden thought, eyeing her handsome date.

She admired the broad set of his shoulders in the tuxedo jacket, his perfectly even bow tie. His hair, playfully falling over his forehead, and his enviably thick eyelashes shielding those gemstone eyes from view.

She still wore her dress and shoes, the wrap covering her bare shoulders, but she'd discarded her purse on the kitchen counter.

A golden glow came from a floor lamp, the only other illumination in the room from the flickering fire. The woods beyond the living room windows were dark and quiet, no wildlife peeking through the trees tonight.

"You're right. Your house is a much better venue for a New Year's Eve party."

Tate approached her with the slow, intentional steps of a predator hunting its prey. "Sorry, I'm only available for private parties."

He lifted one of her hands and with his palm cupped her hip, moving close to rest his cheek on hers. Then he began to sway.

"Are you dancing with me? To no music at all?" she asked, moving with him.

He continued the steps and smoothly spun with her in a slow circle before bringing her flush with his chest. "How's my driving?"

"You're doing great," she whispered into his ear, pleased when a shake ran down his arms. It was nice to know she affected him the same way he affected her—to the *marrow*.

"I owe you for leaving. It wasn't fair of me to ask."

She stopped their silent dance and pulled her cheek from his. "I had to talk to a few people I don't particularly like. I can imagine it'd be upsetting to deal with someone you loathe."

His eyebrows jumped. "You have no idea."

"As long as you reserved plenty of energy for me—" she smoothed the crease above the bridge of his nose "—then I'll overlook you whisking me out of there."

A hint of challenge tightened his jaw. "Are you questioning if I'd keep my word about the champagne kisses and fireside romance?"

"Of course not." She feigned innocence. "I'm simply reminding you that you made promises and that there's no room for waning energy."

He tilted his hips, a hardening part of his anatomy nestling gently into her belly. "Does that feel *waning* to you, Ms. Green?"

She rested her top teeth on her bottom lip, going for her most demure and sex kitten–ish expression.

Then she decided, *screw* demure.

She stroked his erection over his tuxedo pants. He grunted, and she rubbed him again. "Feels positively *mouthwatering* to me," she said against his lips. "But there's only one way to truly test that theory."

He crushed his mouth into hers, pulling away after she was breathless.

"Then test it," he commanded.

Fisting her wrap, he yanked it from her shoulders, sending chills along her back as the lacy material tickled its way down her arms. His grin was slow and sensual and enough to make her drop to her knees right then and there. He stopped her from sinking to the floor, though, his hands cupping her elbows. "Hang on."

On the other side of the room he opened a trunk, pulling from it a rug of faux deer pelts. He spread the blanket in front of the fireplace—large enough that if it *had been* a real deer, it'd have been the size of an elephant—and then threw a few pillows on top of their makeshift bed.

"I don't want you to be cold or uncomfortable." He returned to her embrace.

"Such a gentleman," she cooed.

"Not always."

"Do show me, Mr. Duncan, how ungentlemanly you

can be." She loved the take-charge part of him whenever it came out, and tonight she wanted to play.

He reached into her hair and felt for the pins holding it back, and one by one tossed them to the floor. One, two, three… Her hair spilled from its updo, and then he swept it off her face and gathered it into a ponytail at the back of her head. Tightening his hold, he pulled her head back and lowered his lips to her neck. Teasing and suckling, he worked his way from her throat to her jaw to the sensitive skin behind her ear. "On your knees, gorgeous."

But when he backed away, there was a tickle of a smile on his lips and a question in his eyes, asking if she was okay with this. And since she was very much okay with him being in charge of her—heart and body—she replied, "Yes, sir," and then did as she was told.

Against Tate's chest, Hayden let out a satisfied hum, her breath coasting over his body as she snuggled against him.

After she'd blown his mind and he'd in return happily blown hers, he discarded the condom in the nearest bathroom and grabbed a shearling throw off the couch to cover them. They'd been lying here ever since, the fire warming them—as if they'd needed any help after the amazing sex they'd had.

"Ten point oh" were the first words out of her mouth.

"What's that?"

"The score on your stellar performance." She grinned up at him with sheer sexual satisfaction.

He put an arm behind his head, proud. "You were keeping score?"

"Not really, but I can't deny you any less than perfect, considering it's all I've thought about since we stopped."

He loved satisfying her. Loved more that she was open and forthright about complimenting him.

After the night he'd had, the unpleasant run-ins with both Casey—*the prick*—and Claire, Tate hadn't wanted to ruin Hayden's night, too. Bringing her back to his place was the best decision he could've made.

"What about me?" she asked, raising her eyebrows. "What's my score?"

He pretended to think about it, turning his eyes up to the ceiling. "Eleven million." Her husky laughter drifted over him and he added, "Point eleven."

Her eyes were soft, dreamy.

"Happy new year, Hayden." He was about to apologize for missing the countdown…and forgetting his own promise of champagne, but what she said next stole the remaining oxygen from his lungs.

"I love you, Tate."

He blinked, stunned to his core.

Love.

She loved him. That took living dangerously to an entirely new level.

"I've been in love with you since London. I think." Her nose scrunched in a cute look of consideration. "Probably sooner."

The throw, Hayden's body heat and the fire were suddenly making him overly warm. He threw the blanket off himself, but she only snuggled closer.

"It's hard to know how to tell you've *completely* fallen for someone," she said conversationally as sweat pricked Tate's armpits. "I wasn't planning on falling for you. But I did. So, here we are."

Here we are.

Her tone was playful and light and questioning at the same time. For good reason. When someone told you they loved you, the expected response was to say it back. That was the deal.

That's how it'd been with his and Claire's relationship. Hell, he didn't even remember who'd said it first, only that one of them had and the other had followed suit. Tate had been the one to propose. At a fancy restaurant while wearing a suit, with a ring in a velvet box. He'd done everything by the letter, exactly the way tradition insisted he should, and she'd walked away anyway. Walked away and become someone else's fiancée, before finding an interest in the very part of his life she'd been ambivalent about the entire time she and Tate were together.

In life he'd assumed the next step would naturally appear above the last. That he'd climb one and then ascend to the next. One step up after the last was how he'd built this community on Spright Island, how he'd handled his business dealings. How he'd acted every day of his life…up until the day he bumped into Reid Singleton at that coffee shop.

Life had no rulebook.

What he'd thought was firm footing leading to the next step up had instead been a chute spiraling him down into the darkness, where he'd felt as lost as if he'd worn a permanent blindfold.

Discovering his twin brother.

Finding out he was kidnapped.

Learning about his biological parents in London.

Realizing that his adoptive parents had been wary of the agency from which he was adopted...

Then there was Hayden.

Beautiful, strong, trusting, giving Hayden.

She'd been his confidante and true friend, the woman of his sexual fantasies come true.

And now she loves me.

In what might be the worst timing in the world, Hayden Green had fallen for him, and he had nothing to offer her except metaphors for what he thought life was...and wasn't.

Given enough space he could easily fall in love with Hayden. Hell, if he did a deep-dive into his emotions, he might find he already had. But in no way was he ready for a next step—not with anyone. Claire had reminded him of that tonight.

Hayden deserved a man who knew he loved her without pause or breaking into a cold-hot sweat. After meeting the family who'd put her second her entire life, Tate knew Hayden deserved a man who could put her first.

He wasn't that man.

Not with a hundred other things fighting for first place. His community. Two sets of parents and extended family. His own sense of identity.

Tate had a loose idea about where he was headed and a truckload of physical affection to shower upon her. But an engagement ring and a future?

He swiped the sweat now beading on his brow. He wasn't ready. Not yet.

At the start of this evening, he'd been sure how tonight would go. He'd planned on kissing Hayden at midnight, drinking champagne as gold and silver confetti fluttered to the floor, and then bringing her back here and having sex in front of the fireplace. But only half that plan had come to fruition. He hadn't prepared for bumping into Casey or Claire, or learning that the two of them were business partners.

He'd been building a mountain out of surprise molehills lately, so it shouldn't come as a shock that Hayden had blindsided him with a proclamation of love.

His heart sank.

This was his fault. He'd leaned on her and let her take on his emotional baggage—he'd lavished her with physical love and flew her first-class. Tonight was a Cinderella story right down to the clock striking midnight.

He moved her gently from his chest, ignoring her when she asked where he was going. He reached for his pants and checked his phone. 12:15 a.m. Close enough.

He turned to face Hayden. Beautiful Hayden, with her mussed hair, holding the blanket over her naked body. She was ethereal and perfect and the most sensually attractive woman he'd ever spent time with.

And Tate?

He was the asshole about to break her heart.

Twenty-Three

It didn't take long for Hayden realize that the "I love you" she'd thrown out after Tate's innocent "Happy new year" hadn't gone over well. She didn't know what she expected, but she knew what she'd hoped for.

She'd hoped for one of his easy smiles. She'd hoped he'd thread his fingers into her hair and look deeply into her eyes. She'd hoped for those coveted words—"I love you, too."

She wouldn't have minded if his "I love you" had also included a lengthy explanation of how gobsmacked he was by her announcement.

But this…he looked like he'd witnessed an accident. Panic had surfaced on his features, and he'd become instantly fidgety.

So, yeah, it hadn't gone over well.

"Oh-kay, so that was awkward," she said with an

uneasy laugh. "What I *meant* to say was 'Happy new year to you, too!'"

Her heart beat out a clumsy, erratic rhythm. She hadn't fallen in love with someone in a really, really freaking long time. And this time felt more real, more grounded. She knew who she was and what she wanted. She knew who she loved.

"Claire was at the party tonight." He stood and stuffed his legs into his tuxedo pants.

"Pardon?" Surely she hadn't heard that correctly.

"Claire Waterson. My ex-fiancée."

"I know who Claire is." What she hadn't wrapped her head around yet was that Claire was…at the party?

"She's engaged. And for some reason in a business partnership with Casey." Tate's teeth were all but gnashing.

If Hayden understood what he was saying, his evening had gone south not because of a run-in with Casey, but a visit from Claire…who was *engaged*.

"You didn't tell me she was there," Hayden said.

Hands on his hips, Tate looked down at where she sat on the blanket. "I didn't want to ruin your evening."

"But we left," she reminded him. "*She's* why we didn't stay?"

"It doesn't matter why we left."

But oh, it so did. She'd said I love you and instead of "I love you, too," Tate had told her that his ex-fiancée was engaged to someone else. As if that was the takeaway for the evening. The highlight of tonight!

"We had a special night planned," he explained. "I knew if you saw her it would derail those plans."

Wow.

So Claire had been at the party, had walked over to tell him she was engaged and instead of Tate coming to Hayden and telling her his screwy ex-fiancée was in the building and had apparently moved way, *way* on, he hadn't told Hayden anything. He let her believe that he'd been rankled by that Casey guy, then Tate had swept her up with his handsome smile and wooed her with promises of champagne and making love…

He'd lied by omission. And Hayden was the most honest she'd ever been.

"Let me get this straight…" Hayden heard the shake in her voice. "You thought if I saw Claire tonight, that your chances of getting laid would go way down."

"What? No."

Hayden didn't wait for another of his explanations. She riffled through her discarded clothes and clumsily pulled on her bra and panties.

"Hayden, wait. Don't get dressed."

"I'm not arguing with you naked." She jerked on her sparkly dress, angry that she had nothing else to wear. This was hardly a time for celebrating.

"We're not arguing." When he noticed she was fumbling with her zipper, he offered to help, but she swung away from him.

She raced into the kitchen for her purse, but only when she lifted her coat off the chair did she realize she was stranded. She didn't drive herself tonight.

"Can we talk about this, please?" He snatched his shirt off the couch and pulled it over his shoulders, leaving it open in the front. She admired him, dammit, even while angry with him. He was handsome with his hair a disaster and his shirt open, revealing flat washboard abs, the legs of his pants falling to bare feet that were as attractive as the rest of him.

"There's nothing to talk about. You're still clearly in love with Claire if the news of her engagement hit you so hard you had to leave the party. I'm the moron who thought your heart would be as available as the rest of your body parts!"

"That's not true!" Tate actually shouted, the sound bouncing off the high ceilings and ringing off the light fixture over the dining room table where they stood on opposite sides in a faceoff. "Can we please talk about this?"

"There's nothing to say. I shouldn't have told you… what I told you." She couldn't say those three words to him—even in reference. She should've known better. "I'd been planning on telling you this evening and I thought—"

"You'd been planning this?" But he didn't sound flattered or even appreciative. He sounded *distraught*. "For how long?"

"It doesn't matter. It's clear you don't feel the same way about me." Try as she might, she wasn't able to keep her chin from trembling. This was a nightmare. A waking, living, breathing nightmare. She was in love with him, and not only didn't he know how to tell her he didn't feel the same way, but he'd sort of lied to her tonight, too.

"It's not that. I could… Given enough time. I think." His eyebrows arched sympathetically. Meanwhile, she'd be over here dying of humiliation.

Never had she been this hurt. This disappointed. Not even when her parents had skipped her high school graduation to rescue her grandmother from yet another midday bender.

"The timing is off," Tate said. "That's all this is."

"Oh, is that *all*?" She bit down hard and willed the tears currently tingling behind her eyes not to come. "Tell me, Tate, when is the perfect time for your girlfriend to tell you she loves you? For that matter, when's the perfect time for you to find out you have a secret brother? Or an entire family, for that matter!"

Anger brought forth the tears she'd been swallowing down. Angry at herself for so many reasons, she swept them away with her fingers.

"We can still—"

"Sleep together?" she interrupted before letting out a humorless laugh. "I bet you'd love that. Oh, sorry. I bet you'd *enjoy* that. Let's not use the L-word."

He stalked toward her, his face reddening with anger of his own. A muscle in his jaw ticked, and she felt that win all the way down to her toes. She'd rather him be mad at her than frozen with panic like he'd been earlier.

"I'm not saying the timing has to be perfect," he said. "I just need things to slow down for one goddamn second!"

He pulled his hands over his face like he was startled that he'd yelled, and then calmer, tried again. "I tried to live dangerously. I tried my life being in complete disarray. It didn't work."

Disarray? Danger? Was he referring to their relationship, or was he blaming Hayden for bringing disorder to his life? Was he longing for Claire? The perfect Stepford wife?

"I've worked hard my entire life to keep things

steady," he said. "To achieve incrementally and move my life toward the finish line. The...*situation* with my family has made me question everything I thought I knew about myself. Learning that Claire was engaged threw me, but not because I want her for myself. She was another in a line of failures I couldn't prevent."

Hayden blinked, finally understanding. "And you don't want to be responsible for failing where I'm concerned. So you're not taking the chance? You tried to live dangerously, to give yourself over to the experience that was me, and now I'm not worth the risk."

"You don't understand."

"I understand perfectly. You're too scared to take the chance to love me. I thought you were lost. I didn't know you were a coward."

It was like his blue eyes went up in flames. His complexion darkened, his voice the low warning of a lion.

"I can't meditate and make my problems go away! I *am* Spright Wellness Community." He jabbed his breastbone with one finger. "I'm responsible for an entire community of people. I have to focus. I have to implement actual decisions and strategies that affect others. Even when my life was falling down around me, I kept this place going. Everything I do is in service to the legacy I built. This place will house generations to come. Throughout every bit of adversity I've faced, SWC has thrived. Casey Huxley was a warning that my island could be on shaky ground. I have to be responsible, Hayden. I have to live up to the unbelievable pressures of being the perfect environmental oasis for the families who live here. I'm not a coward. I'm a goddamn saint."

"A saint who is putting work before me!" Hayden shouted, her exposed heart burning with the realization. Another person she loved putting her in second place.

"Yes, exactly!" Tate threw his arms wide before ramming his hands into his hair. "I *can't* put you first! You deserve it and I can't do it."

"It's not like you're housing the homeless, Tate. This is a luxury community. You dwell in a mansion on top of a hill! And who cares what others expect from you? Your 'community' doesn't need you to survive. It can go on without you, you know. You're the asshole with a god complex."

His upper lip curled, the silence stretching between them like a band about to snap. Had she pushed him too far?

"Tell me, Hayden, all the ways you've sacrificed your own needs to take care of the people who need you."

Her ears rang like an explosion had gone off next to her. The words were like a sharp, stinging slap to the cheek. More tears fell, but she didn't feel them. She only knew they were there when they splashed onto her folded arms.

Realization dawned on his face so fast it was dizzying.

"I'm sorry." He stepped closer, and she skirted him and collected her shoes. "I didn't mean—"

"Take me home. *Now*." She slipped on her shoes and pulled her wrap over her shoulders protectively. If only it were an invisible cape.

"Hayden, give me a chance to…" He followed her to

the front door. "That was… I'm angry, okay? I spoke without thinking."

"Now, please." She wouldn't allow Tate to make her feel guilty over a situation he'd never understand. She'd worked hard to untangle herself from her family's co-dependent strings.

Besides, she was beginning to believe that she and Tate weren't good together. This argument had proven that they had a knack for exposing the other's soft underbelly.

She'd been open and honest with him. Now he was using that honesty against her, which made her feel as if she were slowly suffocating.

"Hayden—"

"I have some meditating to do, and I'd prefer to be at home when I do it." Their gazes locked, and she tried not to see the human part of him. Tried to hate him for being cruel and elusive. But she couldn't. She loved him too damn much.

She couldn't stay and continue loving him, not when he didn't love her. With sex in the mix, it would border masochism.

And she refused to linger and hope that one day the timing would be right. That he'd return her feelings when life settled down. Life didn't settle down. Life *was* change—it was a series of bumps and hills, not flat, even plains.

With a tight nod of acquiescence, Tate finished dressing and put on his coat. He shut off the fireplace and scraped his keys from the kitchen counter, walking past Hayden without a second look.

"I'll warm up the car. Come out when you're ready," he said over his shoulder.

Once the door was shut, she looked out the wide picture window into the dark woods beyond.

Like the cold, still landscape, she was empty and alone. As if she'd traded places with that earlier version of Tate who'd stood outside her studio lost, and soaking in the rain.

Twenty-Four

At her front door, her hand resting on the knob, Hayden read the black-and-silver frosting on the sheet cake. "'Happy retirement, Roger'?"

"A mistake," Arlene said, her normally huge blond waves pulled neatly into a ponytail at the back of her head. "Rodger's name is actually spelled with a *D*, or so the lady at Blossom Bakery told me. This was the only cake available on such short notice."

"Why are you bringing me cake?" Hayden stepped aside and Arlene bustled in, a tote and her purse slung over her shoulder.

She'd called Arlene the morning after the New Year's Eve debacle at Tate's house, and Arlene had promised to be right over with "reinforcements."

"I assumed you'd show up with Emily and a few tubs of ice cream." Hayden shut her front door.

"Emily is with *Josh*," Arlene paused for a meaningful eyebrow waggle. "And ice cream is cliché." She pulled a bottle of sparkling wine out of the tote. "I also have hummus, pretzel chips, brie, salmon and lots of those really fattening buttery crackers we love but know are bad for us."

Hayden offered a wan, though grateful, smile. "Don't ruin your resolutions on my account."

"Pfft. Please. It's not too early to crack this open, right?" Arlene asked rhetorically as she tore the foil from the neck of the wine.

"Three o'clock is well within the day-drinking window."

"I'm so sorry I wasn't closer, or I'd have been here sooner." Arlene had been in Seattle when Hayden called her and had promised to come ASAP.

"It's fine. What were you doing, anyway?"

"I was doing a *very* fine younger bodybuilder type named Mike."

Hayden's eyebrows rose.

"I snapped a pic in the shower when he wasn't looking. Want to see?" But her friend's smile fell when Hayden's eyes filled with tears. Arlene quickly put down the bottle and ran to hug her. "I'm sorry. Sorry, sorry," she soothed as she rubbed Hayden's back. "It's too soon for me to be bragging about my hot hookup. And forget about Emily and Josh."

Hayden let out a watery laugh. "It's not too soon. I want you both to be happy."

Arlene leveled her with a look. "I wore my yoga gear so you could torture me in the studio. Whatever makes you feel better."

That did make Hayden laugh. "Yoga's about being kind to yourself, not about torture."

"Whatever you say. Cake first, though. I insist."

Half a sheet cake later, Hayden and Arlene sagged on the sofa, their champagne glasses in hand.

"After that much sugar, you'd think I'd have more energy." Hayden stabbed her plastic fork into the remaining cake. They hadn't bothered with plates. Arlene found two plastic forks left over from takeout and brought them to the couch with the wine and the cake.

It'd been therapeutic to eat her way through half of Rodger's retirement cake, but Hayden still felt the hum of loss in her bones. Arlene knew, though, and like any good best friend did, offered practical advice.

"In Tate's defense, I can imagine his life feels like it's been shaken vigorously and then tumbled out like Yahtzee dice. Can you imagine the combination of joy and disappointment and terror and…I don't know, weirdly, probably peace, he must feel at knowing he has a brother and an entirely new family?"

"His whole life changed. In a blink." Like hers. She hadn't expected to ring in the new year with a breakup *or* a relationship. A few months ago she assumed she'd be working round the clock to accommodate January visitors who'd made resolutions to get fit for the new year.

"Regardless—" Arlene pulled her chin down and gave Hayden a stern stare "—you can't keep your love on ice and wait for Tate to come around. If he has stuff to work through, that's on him. Nobody puts Baby in a corner." She smiled at the *Dirty Dancing* reference, but Hayden couldn't smile just yet. She'd already used up her one for the day.

"I made a commitment before I moved here that I wasn't going to accept half measures in any relationship—from my family, friends or whoever I happened to date."

"I commend you on that." Arlene raised her glass.

"I also committed to listening to my gut. Which is why I called the woman I leased this building from right after I called you."

"*Why* did you do that?" Arlene winced. "Don't say you're leaving me!"

"I'm not going far. I don't think. I might get a job at a gym rather than have the overhead of a new studio right away. I need to not be *here*. Where I'll run into Tate or read about him in the *Spright Times*," she said of the local printed newsletter that was in the café every month.

"But this is your refuge!" Arlene argued, throwing Hayden's words back at her. "I know you're upset, but are you sure you want to give this place up? We love it here. It's peaceful."

"Not if I'm walking through town panicking over the possibility of running into him."

Arlene nodded in what looked like reluctant agreement. "What did the woman say? About your lease?"

"I don't know. I left her a voice mail. The problem is it's a five-year lease. I can't commit to that any longer. I need to cut that tie first. And figure out the rest as I go. I have a nest egg. I'll be fine." Even though Hayden knew that was true—she would be fine—she didn't want to start over. She didn't want to move. She didn't want to look for a job. But with her heart filleted and lying on a cutting board, she didn't see another option.

"You might feel differently in a few days. Don't do anything rash. What if he calls to talk—"

"I don't want to talk to him."

"Do you think he's in love with that Claire chick?"

"No. I don't. That was the spark that started an argument, not the reason for the argument. The only part that matters is that I love him and he can't love me back. His work means more to him than me, and while I want to tell him that's a crock, there was also a time that I put my work before my family, too."

"That's different and you know it." Arlene leveled her with a firm look. "Your family is detrimental, and you're nothing but good for Tate."

Hayden agreed, but... "I don't want to be here. I wish I could... I don't know. Just disappear for a while."

Arlene sat up. She set down her flute of sparkling wine—they hadn't drunk even half a glass apiece since they'd been eagerly wolfing down sheet cake—and stood from the sofa. "Let's go then."

"Let's?"

"Yes! I have frequent flyer miles and some vouchers from work for a free stay at Caesars Palace. You want to get away, and lucky for you, since I went in for the last holiday, my boss owes me. She even said, 'You can have a few extra days off whenever you need. Just let me know.'"

"Caesars Palace? In Vegas?"

Arlene was already tapping the screen of her iPhone.

"Well, I ain't talking about going to Rome, honey." Then into the speaker she said, "Amy, hi. It's Arlene…"

While Arlene paced the width of Hayden's living room explaining to her boss that she'd be out for a few days, a smile Hayden didn't know she had hidden away pulled her cheeks.

Maybe this was what she needed in order to think straight. A few days of being somewhere that was the total antithesis to Spright Island. A loud, smoky, hectic environment where she couldn't sit still and lick her wounds. What had Tate said? That he'd tried living dangerously for a while? Well maybe it was time for her to do the same.

Leaving for a few days was only a matter of packing a bag and rescheduling a few classes. Tate might've convinced himself that this community couldn't survive without him, but she knew they could live without yoga classes for a couple of days.

She was in no shape to be teaching anyone this week, anyway—especially if she spotted Tate walking by or, heaven forbid, if he came in. No one needed to witness her screaming at him, or worse, *blubbering* in the middle of king dancer pose.

"Done." Arlene swiped her phone's screen. "Now for the flight. How soon do you want to leave?"

Hayden crushed Arlene into a hug. A vacation was exactly what she needed. Time to recoup and think about her choices. Maybe Arlene was right and a few days later she wouldn't leave her beloved home. Only time would tell. "Thank you."

"Oh, honey. You know I have your back." All business, Arlene disentangled Hayden from her neck and tapped her phone again. "How soon?"

"As soon as humanly possible."

"That's my girl," Arlene said with a grin.

Tate had promised to entertain his adoptive parents when they came in on January 2, so in spite of not being up to having company, he was resigned to keep his word. Especially since he had skipped Christmas with them to fly to London and spend it with the Singletons.

His mother, Marion, hadn't acted as if it'd bothered her but his father, William, mentioned she'd been sad over the holidays without their normal traditions. Tate loved his parents, and he hadn't been the most receptive son since finding out the news that he was *someone else's* son, too, so he decided to keep his chin up for their sakes—regardless of his tumultuous emotional state.

Which he was determined to compartmentalize.

After dinner at Brass Pony, Tate drove by Hayden's yoga studio, taking note of the closed sign. Her upstairs windows were dark, but it was after nine, so maybe she'd turned in early.

After their argument on New Year's Eve, he'd given her space the next day. It'd nearly killed him not to text or call and apologize or ask that she forgive him— though *begging* might not be out of the question. But he'd been where she was before—angry, bewildered, confused. She had expectations and he'd failed her miserably.

This morning he'd keyed in two texts. One: I'm sorry

and another: Let's talk. Both had gone unanswered, and he supposed he deserved that. She was angry. She had a right to be. She'd professed her love for him, and he'd sat there like a dope.

After Claire's pop-up appearance, his only thought was to get Hayden the hell out of there. His ex showing up at the café had nearly ruined his and Hayden's beginning, and he'd be damned if she'd trumpet in the end.

As much as he wanted to blame his ex for ruining his relationship, though, he couldn't. The fault lay squarely on him. The problem was his inability to be honest with himself, or Hayden. He'd been trying to compartmentalize and control different facets of his life. His head over here in this box, his heart in that one. He was beginning to see it wasn't working. There were no "compartments." There was only him— the whole him.

Marion chattered away about how stuffed she was and how delicious dinner was. "The cheesecake wasn't necessary, Tate." She cradled a plastic takeaway box on her lap in the front seat of his car.

"You mentioned that turtle cheesecake was on the menu fourteen times, Mom." From the corner of his eye, he watched her smile.

"Yes, but my diet…"

"You're beautiful," William said to his wife, squeezing her shoulder. "I tell her that every day," he explained to Tate. "She doesn't believe me. I don't know how many times I have to say 'I love you' and 'you're beautiful' for her believe me."

"Only about a million more times," she answered, patting William's hand.

Dread settled over Tate like a dark cloud. The five-star cuisine in his stomach churned. He reached into his pocket for a red-and-white-striped peppermint candy, unwrapped one end using his teeth and popped the candy into his mouth.

"Are you okay?" his mother asked.

"Ate too much," he told her, but it wasn't true. His throat was full like there was a lump in it and it wasn't from the ahi tuna bowl he'd enjoyed for dinner. He hadn't even had a cocktail, choosing water with a slice of lemon instead. No, he wasn't okay. He was negotiating with grief…or maybe worry was more accurate. He reminded himself for the millionth time that just because they'd argued didn't mean Hayden was gone forever. She was just unreachable at the moment.

In his driveway, he slowed to open the garage door and parked inside. Once his family was in the house, his mother stowed her cheesecake in the fridge "for later," and his father went for the whiskey cabinet to see what was available.

Tate watched them interact with easy smiles and the playful elbow to the ribs he'd often seen his mother give his father. They were in love. It was painfully obvious and not exactly the sort of behavior he'd welcomed as a teenager. He remembered when he was a teenager, rushing his friends off to another part of the house when William and Marion started making out in the kitchen.

"Here you go, son." His dad handed over Tate's drink. "I'm going to watch football. You coming?"

"Yeah. Let me just… In a minute."

William bypassed the dining room and the fireplace where Tate had laid Hayden down two nights ago. In the attached family room, the television clicked on, the sounds of cheering and announcers infiltrating the space.

"Okay." Marion climbed onto one of the bar stools at the breakfast bar and folded her hands. "Why don't you pour me a glass of wine to go with your cocktail and we'll talk about it."

Marion and William Duncan were well into their fifties. Both shorter than Tate, he remembered noting how obvious it was that he was adopted when he'd shot up to six two at age seventeen. Marion's dark hair was cut medium and circling her face. Her cheeks were rosy and round and, despite her suggestion that she needed to lose ten pounds, was on the slim side.

William had a belly, suggesting he liked to eat, and was losing his hair, something that Tate wouldn't have to worry about given George Singleton's full head of hair. But that was a simple matter of DNA and genes passed down—scientific markers of who he was.

Whether or not he was taller than Marion and William, or didn't share their body types didn't matter. Marion and William knew her son. Tate had been living with them from age three and a half until he flew the nest.

In short, they were his parents. They loved him. And his mother could help him through this if he would let her.

"Her name is Hayden" was where he started the story. And since it was a long one, he rounded the bar and sat down before sharing the whole sordid tale.

Twenty-Five

Tate's parents stayed for breakfast and then they were off to catch their plane to San Francisco. The second they were out the door, Tate told himself he needed coffee, but he knew once he left his house and pointed in the direction of the café, he'd drive by Hayden's once more.

Damn.

The closed sign was still hanging on the door of the yoga studio. This was the third day in a row.

At the risk of being accused of being a stalker, or at the very least a heartsick moron, he decided to park and try knocking on her front door.

Last night he'd told Marion everything about Claire. About Hayden. About the trip to London. As the old black-and-white gangster movies his dad liked to watch were known for saying, Tate had sung like a canary.

It bubbled out of him in one messy, winding story, and by the end he was mortified to find himself hunkered over his drink, his eyes burning with unshed tears and his liquor untouched.

But his mother had never expected him to ignore his emotions, so he didn't.

"It's too much to handle. I just need time," he'd said in frustration, finally taking a burning swallow of the whiskey his father had poured for him.

His mother's hand rubbed his back as she hummed thoughtfully to herself.

"That's what you've got for me?" he asked. "A thoughtful hum?"

Knowing he was teasing her, Marion's mouth curved at the edge. "I'm not sure if you want me to tell you you're wrong or not. Should I agree instead?"

He'd had to admit he could use some female insight, so he answered his mother's question with one of his own.

"How am I wrong?" The question came out with a frustrated edge, so he took another swallow from his glass. "What the hell was I supposed to do when everything was thrown at me in rapid succession?"

Another thoughtful hum came from Marion. "Be honest with yourself, and then be honest with Hayden."

"I was!"

"You *weren't*. You acted as if you don't know how to feel." Marion shook her head. "That's bull, Tate. You know. You're afraid to admit it, but you know."

He'd opened his mouth to argue, but he couldn't. She was right.

Last night he'd gone to bed and had slept three,

maybe four hours on and off. He'd tossed and turned and rationalized and thought through, around and over everything he and his mother had talked about.

He was in love with Hayden. Of course he was. She'd taken as much of him as she'd given of herself, and when she'd been vulnerable, he'd offered a lame excuse about *timing*.

He woke with a panicky feeling, an unease unlike any he'd felt before. He knew what he had to do, and for once, making the decision to confess how badly he'd fucked up seemed easy.

Upstairs, at Hayden's apartment door, Tate ignored the fullness of his heart, now lodged in his throat, and knocked. He waited. Knocked again. No answer.

"Hayden? If you're in there, I just need a few seconds." He braced his palms on the doorframe and waited. Nothing. "I have something to say and it has to be in person. Sixty seconds, tops."

He needed her to listen to what he had to say. He couldn't let another moment pass with her believing that he'd prioritized everyone and everything in his life over her—over the woman he loved.

"How about thirty seconds?" He could work with thirty. He just needed her to open the damn door.

Pulling his phone from his pocket, he called her and heard the distinct jingle of her ringtone inside the apartment about one second before he heard the outside door close and the sound of someone coming up the stairs.

"She left her phone at home. She's not here." One of Hayden's friends, the one with the short hair, not the bawdy blonde one, regarded him coolly. "I'm here to water her plants."

"Where is she?" He stepped aside so she could unlock the door and let herself in.

"I'm sure if she wanted you to know that, she would have told you."

She started to shut the door but he stopped it with one hand. "Is she safe?"

"She's safe." Her eyes warmed slightly. "She's with Arlene."

"Arlene. The blonde one." Tate offered a smile, but the brunette only scowled. "Thank you…"

"Emily." She sighed.

"Emily. Thank you. Can you tell me when she'll be back?"

She pressed her lips together.

"Ballpark?" he tried.

"Tomorrow, unless they decide to stay in…*wherever* they went."

"You know though. Where they went."

"Of course I know where they went." She frowned. "I also know that she's seriously considering buying herself out of the lease and leaving Spright Island because of *you*. Do you know how much she loves it here? Can you even fathom what she did to move here? What she gave up? She doesn't own a car, Tate. Not because she's trying to save the planet but because she sunk every dollar she had into her yoga studio. When Hayden goes in, she goes *all in*. Her friends are lifers."

Her lips twisted in consideration as she considered him, and his position in Hayden's life.

"I know I screwed up," he said, still wrapping his

head around the idea that Hayden might leave Spright Island because of him.

"You think?" Emily propped her fist on her hip, not ready to let him off the hook.

"I *know*. I'll do whatever it takes for her to stay."

"Like what? Buy the building?" she snapped.

He smiled, not denying that buying the building was his first instinct. But he wouldn't trap her into staying. He wouldn't trick her into sticking around. She deserved to have the life she built, and he'd honor that.

"No. I'm not going to buy the building. But I promise, I won't be the reason she leaves."

Some of Emily's skepticism fled from her face, compassion replacing it. "This community is better because of her."

Emily was right. He'd seen residents interact with Hayden, the smiles at the café or the restaurant whenever she was around. She was contagious and beautiful. Incredible, really. How had been so obtuse not to see what was right in front of him. Of course Spright Wellness Community was better because of Hayden.

"We all are," he told Emily. And then he turned to leave.

Twenty-Six

Vegas was exactly what Hayden needed, which was surprising to say the least. Normally she focused on being quiet and listening to her inner voice to clear her mind.

In this case a few days of drinks, gambling and a male strip show had cleared her mind just fine.

Arlene dropped Hayden off at her studio, a large pair of dark sunglasses hiding the evidence of a killer hangover. Hayden, while she'd enjoyed a few cocktails, hadn't abused her liver while she was in Vegas. Her drug of choice had been the craps table. She left up forty dollars, which she considered a win since she'd been down over two hundred bucks before that. She knew when to cut and run.

Apparently.

"I'm going to go home and die," Arlene said, droll.

"I have detox tea upstairs if you think it would help."

"Not sure anything would help except maybe a time machine. Then I could undrink those last four margaritas."

Hayden had been swamped with regret during the flight home to Washington, which made Arlene's next question easy to answer.

"Are you seriously moving off Spright Island?" Arlene looked sad to ask it, which warmed Hayden's heart. She truly loved her friends.

"Of course not."

"Yes!" Arlene shouted before clutching her head with both hands. "Ow, my skull."

"Go home. Get some sleep. And thank you for a fantastic trip."

She stepped out of the car and Arlene drove away. It was cool, but sunny, and Hayden paused to take in the market across the street, waving at Sherry who'd just pulled open the door to walk in.

All around her there were smiling faces, and beautiful trees. Homes and retail establishments that were cared for and well-loved.

Spright Island and the people who lived here were Hayden's salvation. No matter what happened between her and Tate in the future, she wouldn't rob herself of the joy of living here. She was a better person here and this community—a place that Tate had envisioned into all its glory—was special. She sucked in a lungful of crisp air and turned, alarmed to see the man of her thoughts standing on the sidewalk outside her studio.

That speech had sounded fine inside her head. Faced

with him, however, her instincts told her to protect herself. Build that wall as high and strong as she could.

"Hayden."

That voice.

Tate had said her name in every way imaginable. During the throes of heated sexual contact, in jest, when he was angry or happy. She heard compassion in his voice now; saw it on his face, too. He regretted their argument, that much was clear. But if he didn't love her—when she still loved him with everything she was—then nothing had changed except the date.

"Hi."

"Can I talk to you?" he asked.

She didn't want to talk to him. Not yet. Not until... Until what? Until she fell out of love with him? Who knew how long that would take.

Willing herself to be brave, she called up the very strength of character that brought her to Spright Wellness Community in the first place. "Sure."

"May I?" He gestured to her carry-on and she nodded, letting him take the luggage as she unlocked her studio door. She tried to ignore the brush of his hand on hers and the soft scent of leather coming off his coat. She tried, but failed.

Mere days ago she could've greeted him with a kiss. A hug. Maybe more. It was hard to believe after all they'd experienced together—with his family and hers—that this was over.

Stepping into her yoga studio, she focused instead on its pale wood floors and salt lamps. The padded blocks and yoga mats and water bottles for sale.

No way would she abandon her dream any more

than Tate would abandon his. She hadn't run away from her family or her responsibility when she left Seattle. She'd run *toward* a dream—a vision that burned in her heart. There was a difference.

"I heard you were considering leaving," he said, flipping the lock behind him.

So they were doing this here.

"Where'd you hear that?"

"Emily. But don't be upset with her. She told me that so I'd know where her loyalty lies. With you. She doesn't want you to leave." He took a long, slow look around her studio. "No one at Spright Island wants you to leave. *I* don't want you to leave."

It was great to hear that. She wanted to shout with joy! But just because he didn't want her to leave didn't mean he was suddenly and madly in love with her, did it?

"I'm not leaving," she said cautiously.

"Good." His smile caused an ache in her heart she was sure would drop her to her knees. So she flexed her core to keep her standing and folded her arms to protect herself. It wasn't a wall, but it was all she had. She wanted to believe that everything had changed. That he'd recalled their fight with the regret she felt whenever she thought about it. That he wished as much as she did that they had stopped and put their egos on hold long enough to have a conversation about what it meant to be together—and just how much they meant to each other.

It might not have salvaged what they had—she wasn't accepting less than she deserved from anyone— but they could've ended things amicably.

He stepped deeper into the room and came as close as he could without touching her. So close she had to tilt her head back to look up at him.

"I love you, Hayden. I fell in love with you probably before you fell for me, but I was too busy compartmentalizing and trying to sort out everything to realize it. I *should've* realized it. Nothing has ever been clearer than the fact that you belong with me and I already belong to you. I handled that night by the fireplace so badly. I messed up."

She felt her mouth drop open and she stood there in stunned silence combing over everything he'd said. He'd…fallen in love with her?

"I'm sorry," he continued. "For everything I said that night that was unfair and untrue. For making you think for one second you mattered less to me than anything on this planet."

She still couldn't speak so she stood there, mute as a mime as Tate reached into his jacket pocket and came out with his phone.

"You were thinking of leaving so that you didn't have to run into me, weren't you? So we could avoid each other at the market. Not cross paths while dining in the same restaurant." He tilted his head. "Not bump into each other in the park in the spring."

Yes to all of those things, but that was juvenile, wasn't it? Trying to avoid him. Tate Duncan *was* Spright Island.

"We'll work it out," she said carefully, still unraveling what he'd said to her. Her heart was grasping to his "I love you," desperate to be healed, but her mind… Her mind was more skeptical.

"I have a proposition for you. If you still love me, I want to be with you without barriers. Without compartments. Without playing it safe. Safe is for pussies."

Half her mouth lifted, hope filling her heart against her will.

He swiped the screen of his phone. "But if you've stopped loving me, or you can't trust me to make good on my promise to love you back, well…"

He offered the cell phone and she took it with shaking hands.

"It's a deed," he explained. "To my new house in San Francisco." He tapped the screen of the phone and brought up a text message with a timestamp from yesterday. "Which means I can sell my house here."

It was from Sherry, the real estate agent. Hayden read it, her eyes heating with tears. *I'm sure we can find the perfect buyer for your house, and fast!*

"You're…leaving?" Spright Island without Tate was as wrong as Hayden's life without Tate. "You love that house."

"I do," he admitted.

"You love it here," she said, emotion tightening her throat.

"I do." He put a hand on her arm and gave her a gentle squeeze. "But not more than I love you. I won't put anything before that."

He plucked the phone from her trembling fingers and pocketed it. "I know you can't see it, but I'm falling apart, Hayden. I miss you every moment you're not here, and hearing that you were considering uprooting what you've built because of—because I was too afraid to be honest with you… It's not right for you to compromise. So I will. For you. You deserve everything you've worked so hard to gain."

He waited while she stared, tears trembling on the edges of her eyelids. His every word had sealed up the crack he'd put in her heart.

He loved her. He *loved* her.

And he wanted her to stay. He was willing to walk away from his legacy and move back to California. He was giving her the community that needed him as much as he'd originally stated.

Silly billionaire.

"If I could rewind that night, we'd stay at the party, and drink champagne at midnight, and I'd kiss you so that everyone there would know what you meant to me. We'd still make love at my house by the fire—" he blew out a breath "—I don't see how that could get any better."

She bit her lip to hide a smile. Neither did she. It'd been everything.

"But you wouldn't have had the chance to tell me you love me, Hayden. Not before I said I loved you first." His eyes shimmered, as if the emotions he'd refused to share with her had pushed their way past his defenses.

"I followed rules my entire life. None of them kept me safe from drama or a broken relationship. When I broke those rules with you, though, I was more whole than I've ever been. My identity was mixed up in parents I'd never met and a twin brother I was getting to know. What I didn't know was that with you, I was becoming someone else. Someone better. I hope…the right man for you." His smile broke through, but nervous like he had no idea how she'd react. She knew, though. She knew. "I love you so much. I don't know where you went, but I know why, and I deserved it. I deserve whatever it is you say next."

He swallowed thickly, straightening his shoulders for the blows that would come. Ready to accept whatever she had to say—ready, if she said the word, to walk away from everything he cared about.

But she loved him. She'd never ask him to do that.

"When I left Seattle behind, when I parted ways from my family, it was to become a better version of myself. The reason I'm not leaving Spright Island isn't because of my yoga studio, or my apartment, or even this amazing community. I'm staying because of who I am when I'm here. I'm better. More caring. More giving. And that has a lot to do with you, Tate Duncan. You're more than this community. You're more than a legacy for generations to come. You're the man I love more than anything." A tear tumbled from her eye. "I'm better when I'm with *you*."

Before she finished speaking, Tate was crushing her against him.

"Thank God," he said into her hair, before lifting her face and seeking her lips with his. One kiss, perfect and sweet, and then he looked down at her with sheer awe.

"You, Hayden, are my legacy. Not this community. I'll never let work, or exes, or family come between us again. Whatever comes up we'll handle it. Together. Forever."

"I like the sound of forever." She wrapped her fingers around his and stood on her tiptoes. "But first, you have to make up for the last few days."

He smiled against her lips. "Name your price."

"Well, there was this strip show I saw…shirtless guys covered in oil…" She ran her hands over his button-down shirt. "How do you look in a g-string?"

He laughed, but frowned when he saw that she was serious. "Really?"

"Maybe. But I definitely will need you to call Sherry and tell her you're not selling your house in the woods."

"Done."

She brushed a lock of dark hair from his forehead. "I see no harm in keeping the house in San Francisco, though. We have to stay somewhere when we visit your parents in California."

He scooped her up against him and kissed away her grin, his mouth exploring hers in a movie-worthy, happy-ever-after kiss before setting her on her feet.

"I love you, Hayden Green."

"I love you, too, Tate Duncan." She tapped her chin. "Or is it Wesley Singleton?"

"Something else for you to decide."

"Me? Why me?"

"I'd like to give you one of those last names soon, along with a wedding ring. And a coveted house in the woods on an island."

Her head spun with possibility, with a future she hadn't dared imagine before this moment.

"What do you think?" he asked.

"I think…that fairy tales do come true."

"Except in this case, you're the one who saved me." Tate gestured to the sidewalk outside her studio. "You pulled me out of the rain, and then you kissed me. And I was never the same."

"Me neither."

"Well, then maybe we saved each other."

"Yeah." She smiled. "Maybe we did."

Epilogue

3 years later

The Duncan-Green wedding had happened last summer. The Commons were transformed for the lavish ceremony, decorated in, lavender and cream.

Hayden's family—the Greens—had attended, on their best behavior without Grandma Winnie in tow. She'd passed away eight months ago now, her suffering meeting its end. Quite a bit of Hayden's and her mother's had died along with Winnie. Both of Tate's families had shown as well—the Duncans and the Singletons—and as a result the Singletons hadn't returned to Spright Island that winter for Christmas.

This year, they had. Christmas dinner had been served in their home—Hayden and Tate's mansion in the woods. They'd proudly stepped Marion and Wil-

liam through the tradition of Christmas crackers, and
Jane and George had gotten their first taste of American holiday cuisine.

Reid and Drew had come to celebrate with them as
well and were currently sitting on the floor with their
two-year-old son, Roland. Drew cooed over her baby
boy, who was tearing apart a box—a box that had previously contained an outfit that Roland was ignoring.

Aunt Hayden understood his lack of excitement.

Tate came into the room with a tray of mugs as Jane
followed with their family's specialty: bread pudding.
Hayden had thought she was too stuffed for another
bite, but now that she saw the rich dessert she knew
she wouldn't be able to deny herself a taste.

"We have one more gift," Tate said after everyone
had settled into the sofas and chairs with their desserts.

"A surprise actually," Hayden said, pulling one last
paper-wrapped Christmas cracker from its hiding place
on the tree.

"Another cracker?" Jane asked.

"A *very special* cracker." Tate took the wrapped gift
from Hayden and handed it to Jane, then gestured to
his Marion. "Mom, why don't you take the other end
and give it a tug."

"Okay, but I'm not reading another silly joke." Marion warned. Her Christmas cracker contained a dirty
joke about Rudolph and his "sleigh balls." Hayden
wasn't sure how it got there, but she thought Reid might
have had something to do with it.

"I promise there is no joke." Hayden tucked her
palms around her protruding belly, excited for the
grandparents to learn what she and Tate now knew.

The pair of moms tugged and the cracker popped, spraying out paper confetti and a rolled photo. Jane reached for it first, gasping as she studied the blurry black-and-white ultrasound.

"You know the sex!" Jane exclaimed, squinting at the blurs and bumps on the photo.

"Let me see!" Marion sat close to Jane and leaned in also.

It took only a few seconds for Jane to recognize what had so obviously been there all along.

"Twins!" Jane exclaimed.

"Twins?" Marion repeated and both women burst into tears.

William and George shook hands and then claimed it was time for celebrating with cigars. Drew left Roland in Reid's arms to see the photo for herself.

"Twins?" Reid frowned at his own son and then to Tate. "Show-off."

Soon after, the bread pudding and coffee were gone. The men went to light cigars in celebration of twin baby boys coming soon to a wellness community near them.

Before Tate went outside with his brother and fathers he made sure to stop and place a kiss on Hayden's lips.

"Merry Christmas, Tate."

"Merry Christmas, Hayden." He bent to press his lips to her tummy then stood and gave her a wink. "And family."

* * * * *

If you loved Tate's story, don't miss the other men of
The Bachelor Pact,
a series from Jessica Lemmon!

Best Friends, Secret Lovers
Temporary to Tempted
One Night, White Lies

COMING NEXT MONTH FROM

HARLEQUIN® *Desire*

Available November 5, 2019

#2695 RANCHER'S WILD SECRET

Gold Valley Vineyards • by Maisey Yates

Holden McCall came to Gold Valley with one goal: seduce his enemy's innocent engaged daughter, Emerson Maxfield. But the tempting cowboy didn't plan for good girl Emerson to risk everything, including her future, to indulge the desire neither can resist...

#2696 HOT HOLIDAY RANCHER

Texas Cattleman's Club: Houston • by Catherine Mann

Rancher Jesse Stevens wants to get married, but Texas heiress Esme Perry is *not* the woman the matchmaker promised. And when they're stranded together during a flash flood—over Christmas—will passion sweep them into something more than a holiday fling?

#2697 THE REBEL

Dynasties: Mesa Falls • by Joanne Rock

Lily Carrington is doubly off-limits to Marcus Salazar: not only is she engaged to another man when she meets the media mogul, but she's also a spy for his business-rival brother. Can Marcus tame his desire for her—and will he want to?

#2698 A CHRISTMAS RENDEZVOUS

The Eden Empire • by Karen Booth

After a chance encounter leads to a one-night stand, lawyers Isabel Blackwell and Jeremy Sharp find themselves reunited on opposite sides of a high-stakes case at Christmas. As their forbidden attraction reignites, her past and a surprise revelation threaten everything...

#2699 SECOND CHANCE TEMPTATION

Love in Boston • by Joss Wood

Years ago, Tanna left Boston businessman Levi at the altar. Now she's back to make amends and move on with her life. Until Levi traps her into staying—and shows her the life she could have had. But their complicated past could destroy their second chance...

#2700 ONE NIGHT, TWO SECRETS

One Night • by Katherine Garbera

Heiress Scarlet O'Malley *thinks* she had a one-night stand with a certain Houston billionaire, but learns it was his twin, Alejandro Velasquez! The switch isn't her only shock. With a baby on the way, can their night of passion last a lifetime?

_____

YOU CAN FIND MORE INFORMATION ON UPCOMING HARLEQUIN® TITLES, FREE EXCERPTS AND MORE AT WWW.HARLEQUIN.COM.

HDCNM1019

Get 4 FREE REWARDS!

We'll send you 2 FREE Books plus 2 FREE Mystery Gifts.

Harlequin® Desire books feature heroes who have it all: wealth, status, incredible good looks... everything but the right woman.

FREE
Value Over
$20

YES! Please send me 2 FREE Harlequin® Desire novels and my 2 FREE gifts (gifts are worth about $10 retail). After receiving them, if I don't wish to receive any more books, I can return the shipping statement marked "cancel." If I don't cancel, I will receive 6 brand-new novels every month and be billed just $4.55 per book in the U.S. or $5.24 per book in Canada. That's a savings of at least 13% off the cover price! It's quite a bargain! Shipping and handling is just 50¢ per book in the U.S. and $1.25 per book in Canada.* I understand that accepting the 2 free books and gifts places me under no obligation to buy anything. I can always return a shipment and cancel at any time. The free books and gifts are mine to keep no matter what I decide.

225/326 HDN GNND

Name (please print)

Address   Apt. #

City   State/Province   Zip/Postal Code

Mail to the **Reader Service:**
IN U.S.A.: P.O. Box 1341, Buffalo, NY 14240-8531
IN CANADA: P.O. Box 603, Fort Erie, Ontario L2A 5X3

Want to try 2 free books from another series? Call 1-800-873-8635 or visit www.ReaderService.com.

SPECIAL EXCERPT FROM

HARLEQUIN®
Desire

*Emerson Maxfield is the perfect pawn for rancher
Holden McCall's purposes. She's engaged to a man
solely to win her father's approval, and the sheltered
beauty never steps out of line. Until one encounter
changes everything. Now this good girl must marry
Holden to protect her family—or their desire could
spell downfall for them all…*

Read on for a sneak peek at
Rancher's Wild Secret
by New York Times *bestselling author Maisey Yates!*

"I'll tell you what," he said. "I'm going to give you a kiss.
And if afterward you can walk away, then you should."

She blinked. "I don't want to."

"See how you feel after the kiss."

He dropped the ax, and it hit the frozen ground with a
dull thump.

He already knew.

He already knew that he was going to have a hard time
getting his hands off her once they'd been on her. The
way that she appealed to him hit a primitive part of him
he couldn't explain. A part of him that was something
other than civilized.

She took a step toward him, those ridiculous high
heels somehow skimming over the top of the dirt and
rocks. She was soft and elegant, and he was half-dressed

and sweaty from chopping wood, his breath a cloud in the cold air.

She reached out and put her hand on his chest. And it took every last ounce of his willpower not to grab her wrist and pin her palm to him. To hold her against him, make her feel the way his heart was beginning to rage out of control.

He couldn't remember the last time he'd wanted a woman like this.

And he didn't know if it was the touch of the forbidden adding to the thrill, or if it was the fact that she wanted his body and nothing else. Because he could do nothing for Emerson Maxfield, not Holden Brown, the man he was pretending to be. The man who had to depend on the good graces of his employer and lived in a cabin on the property. There was nothing he could do for her.

She didn't even want emotions from him.

But this woman standing in front of him truly wanted only this elemental thing, this spark of heat between them to become a blaze.

And who was he to deny her?

Will their first kiss lead to something more
than either expected?

Find out in
Rancher's Wild Secret
by New York Times *bestselling author Maisey Yates.*

Available November 2019 wherever
Harlequin® Desire books and ebooks are sold.

Harlequin.com

Want to give in to temptation with
steamy tales of irresistible desire?

Check out **Harlequin® Presents®,
Harlequin® Desire** and
Harlequin® Kimani™ Romance books!

New books available every month!

CONNECT WITH US AT:

Facebook.com/groups/HarlequinConnection

 Facebook.com/HarlequinBooks

 Twitter.com/HarlequinBooks

 Instagram.com/HarlequinBooks

 Pinterest.com/HarlequinBooks

ReaderService.com

**ROMANCE WHEN
YOU NEED IT**

PGENRE2018

Love Harlequin romance?

DISCOVER.

Be the first to find out about promotions, news and exclusive content!

Facebook.com/HarlequinBooks

Twitter.com/HarlequinBooks

Instagram.com/HarlequinBooks

Pinterest.com/HarlequinBooks

ReaderService.com

EXPLORE.

Sign up for the Harlequin e-newsletter and download a free book from any series at **TryHarlequin.com.**

CONNECT.

Join our Harlequin community to share your thoughts and connect with other romance readers!
Facebook.com/groups/HarlequinConnection

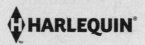

HARLEQUIN®

ROMANCE WHEN YOU NEED IT

HSOCIAL2018

THE WORLD IS BETTER WITH

Romance

Harlequin has everything from contemporary, passionate and heartwarming to suspenseful and inspirational stories.

Whatever your mood, we have a romance just for you!

Connect with us to find your next great read, special offers and more.

f /HarlequinBooks

@HarlequinBooks

www.HarlequinBlog.com

www.Harlequin.com/Newsletters

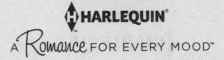

HARLEQUIN®

A *Romance* FOR EVERY MOOD™

www.Harlequin.com

SERIESHALOAD2015